The North Wind Doth Blow

The North Wind Doth Blow

Alan S Watts

ATHENA PRESS
LONDON

THE NORTH WIND DOTH BLOW
Copyright © Alan S Watts 2009

All Rights Reserved

ISBN 978 1 84748 489 5

First published 2009 by
ATHENA PRESS
Queen's House, 2 Holly Road
Twickenham TW1 4EG
United Kingdom

Printed for Athena Press

One: All our company here

Mr Bassenthwaite, landlord of the Packhorse Inn, led the way to his front parlour.

'Beggin' tha pardon, ladies and gentlemen,' he announced, 'but here's a young man makin' enquiries of thee.'

'Enquiries of us?'

Jeremy knew the voice as well as the face.

'Mr Dempsey, isn't it, sir?' he asked.

The dark handsome man with the clear ringing voice looked surprised, then came forward with his hand outstretched.

'It is indeed, my young friend.'

'I recognised you as you came into Penkley on the coach,' explained Jeremy, rather flustered at finding himself in the company of a man he so much admired, and even more so because he was aware of the other actors and actresses looking on.

'See, Mulrooney!' cried Dempsey with enthusiasm. 'Our fame is spread abroad. You have just described this place as god-forsaken, blighted, dirty, and I don't know what – yet here's a lad who recognises us as soon as we show our faces.'

'And that's fame indeed, Mr Dempsey!' returned a short, swarthy man who was leaning on the back of a chair by the fireside. 'To be sure it is! With us wrapped up to our eyes in rugs and ulsters, I wouldn't have thought our own mothers would have known us.'

He took a pace towards Jeremy.

'Your hand, sir. It's good to meet one so young who knows a real actor when he meets one.'

'It was Mr Dempsey I thought I recognised,' stammered Jeremy.

'Aha! You see, Mulrooney! As you so wisely say, he knows a real actor when he sees one!' laughed Dempsey. 'And pray, my young friend, how did you come to know me?'

'I remembered seeing you at Drury Lane.'

'Drury Lane? That must have been a year ago at least.'

'It was. Well before the battle.'

'Battle?'

'I meant the Battle at Waterloo, sir. My father took me to Drury Lane several times to see you. He was killed in the battle.'

There was a sympathetic silence, until Dempsey said, 'I am sorry to hear it, lad!' and placed a kindly hand on his arm. Then he continued, 'But tell me, my fine young friend, you evidently know a great deal about us. It's time we learnt more about you. Your name, young sir. Is it too much to ask?'

'My name…' began Jeremy. At these words he seemed to be back in the London lodgings again, rehearsing scenes with his father who had always, despite his military career, been fond of the stage. ' "My name… my name is Norval. On yonder Grampian heights my father feeds his flocks…" '

At this unexpected quotation of very well-known lines, the company was convulsed with laughter, and Dempsey slapped his thigh and called out: 'Hey, Mulrooney! Here's another Roscius! Master Betty is back again. Just listen to him.'

But from the side of the fireplace came a querulous voice.

'*Master Betty? Master Betty?* We want no more Master Bettys. No more boys at all. And why this boy should intrude upon us, I can't imagine.'

'Oh, come, Henrietta!' pleaded Mr Dempsey. 'The lad came to pay his respects. I think it highly courteous of him.'

'Then let him depart. Whatever you do, James, don't encourage him. One Master Betty was enough for my lifetime. Don't let's have another one, please!'

The speaker was an imperious lady with a hooked nose dominating her features and a great mass of curled hair on the top of her head.

'But the lad shows promise, Henrietta.'

'Promise of what?' she asked. 'I don't believe in boys, especially boys who mouth lines of verse. Let them play whip and top, but keep them off the stage. That Master Betty nearly worked our ruin, remember. Everyone went flocking to gape at him, while professionals such as myself – and Sarah Siddons – were completely ignored. A scandal, if ever there was one.'

'I am sorry, ma'am,' said Jeremy meekly. 'I had no intention of distressing you.'

She rustled her voluminous dress of blue and gold satin.

'I take no offence, young man, so long as you have no ambitions to set foot on the stage.'

'I must confess, ma'am—'

'I knew it!' exclaimed Henrietta, holding up both hands to express her horror and dismay. 'As soon as I saw him, I knew it. He wants to be an actor. Is the theatre to be given over to infant prodigies and freaks? Are all the true actors and actresses – myself, the Kembles, Edmund Kean – to be ignored while these juvenile contortionists perform their tricks! Get rid of the boy at once before he turns your heads!'

'Now, now, Henrietta, I am sure the boy has no such designs.'

'Indeed, no, ma'am,' stammered Jeremy, very much taken aback by the torrents of wrath which poured from the lady's lips. 'Rather, I hold you in the deepest respect for your wonderful acting, Mrs Heller.'

At these words, Mrs Heller's attitude changed at once.

'Ah!' she cooed. 'He recognises me also, James Dempsey! To be sure, the boy can be no mere country clod.' She beamed her most gracious smile.

'Forgive me if I was uncivil, boy,' she said, 'but I haven't thawed out since we descended from the coach. And this fire…'

She turned to the girl standing behind her. 'Go along, child, and tell the landlord we are almost frozen to death. This miserable fire won't last another five minutes if he doesn't fetch more kindling and a pair of bellows.'

The girl was about fourteen, and so like Mrs Heller as to be unmistakeably her daughter. She pushed herself away from the wall with a poor grace, as if she greatly resented being asked to do anything, and was so slow about it that, before she had put one foot in front of the other, Mulrooney had opened the door and called out: 'Landlord! The fire's nearly out!'

'And ask him to bring me a glass of hot brandy and water,' ordered the actress, rustling her great gown like a peacock rustling its feathers. 'What a place, Dempsey! And what discomfort! As if this morning's journey over the hills wasn't enough for one day!'

'The price of our profession, madam,' declared Dempsey. 'We are not, alas, like other mortals. We must perforce roam the wide world like the Wandering Jew, suffer discomfort and privations, never enjoy the security of a home—'

'Dempsey, you talk too much,' declared the grand lady, appealing with her eyes to the ceiling. 'Call the landlord again, Mulrooney. My nose is turning blue and I haven't the least feeling in my fingers.'

She turned to the rest of the company. Besides the four already described, there was a tall, obsequious man, an elderly gentleman with a bald head, and a thin, acid-faced woman.

'Why must everyone be standing about like pieces of scenery?' Mrs Heller demanded. 'Won't your joints bend, Mr Cadwallader? Or yours, Miss Sharp?'

The tall man gave a little smile of submission and helped the thin woman to take a chair. Then he and his colleague also found seats.

'Well, the room looks tidier now,' Mrs Heller began to say when the door opened and the landlord came in with a shovelful of flaming coals. As he crossed to the fireplace, the room was filled with sulphurous fumes.

'No! No!' screamed Mrs Heller. 'You great blundering Lancashire dunderhead! Have you no thought for your guests? Are my lungs to be burnt out?'

The smoke was certainly irritating, making everyone cough.

'Oh, my eyes! My chest!'

Mrs Heller had a tremendous voice when she chose to use it, and when she coughed her coughing was louder than anyone else's.

Dempsey immediately opened the casement, and the others soon recovered. But Mrs Heller continued to cough with so powerful a delivery that Jeremy was convinced she must do herself a permanent injury.

So too was the landlord. He had never expected such repercussions merely from carrying a few hot coals into a room. He stood dumbfounded, staring at Mrs Heller with his mouth wide open.

Fortunately Dempsey ushered him out, whispering to him as he went to remember that the lady had ordered some hot brandy and water. Dempsey then turned to the actress.

'My dear Henrietta, the fire has brightened considerably, and your drink will be here in a moment.'

Mrs Heller recovered in an instant. Giving her eyes a final dab with her cambric handkerchief, she leaned over and warmed her hands at the blaze. When Bassenthwaite returned and the fumes of the brandy assailed her nostrils, she was completely restored.

'Ah!' she said, sipping with obvious enjoyment. 'What a pity you have to be self-denying, James, and can't share my pleasure. But I mustn't tempt you.'

'But it's tempting me you are,' said the Irishman, sniffing at the fragrance. 'And by your leave, 'tis a drop o' something warming I'll be taking meself.'

Bassenthwaite was recalled and drinks ordered for everyone, except Jeremy and Dempsey. Jeremy wondered why Mrs Heller had said that Dempsey had to be self-denying. These were drinking times, and it was unusual for a man to abstain. To Jeremy, brought up in military company, it seemed positively unnatural.

'Now, my young fellow,' said Dempsey, when everyone was accommodated. 'You have yet to introduce yourself.'

'I am Jeremy Blatchford,' he told them. 'I live with my Uncle Reuben, who owns the big mill here. Tankard's New Mill, they call it.'

Dempsey's blue eyes seemed to sharpen at the name 'Tankard', although his smiling expression never changed.

'How is it you saw us in Drury Lane,' he asked, 'when your home is here in a cotton-spinning town?'

'I lived in London until my father's death. Then my uncle adopted me. Last August he came down to London and fetched me up here.'

'Last August? Then you haven't been here very long?'

Jeremy could not help wondering whether this was a deliberate question, or mere polite conversation. There was a shrewd, alert brain behind those blue eyes.

'Not long, sir,' he replied.

'And how do you like the North Country?'

'I don't,' said Jeremy without hesitation. 'The sooner I can get back to London, the better.'

'Now, now,' protested the actor. 'London isn't everything.'

'It's everything to me,' replied the lad, and received approving nods from Mr Cadwallader and Miss Sharp. 'Besides, in London there isn't this feeling all the time... like doom hanging over one.'

'Doom?' asked Dempsey, raising his eyebrows.

'I know it sounds a bit strong,' said Jeremy. 'But that's the only way I can describe it. Although I haven't been here long, I can feel it, just as if there was a big thunderstorm looming up.'

Dempsey smiled. 'Southerners often find the North a bit oppressive,' he said. 'But you'll soon settle down.'

'Somehow I don't think I will,' said Jeremy with a shake of the head. 'I miss London too much. I liked the bustle of all the people. And as for the theatres...'

'There are people and theatres in Manchester and Liverpool,' Dempsey reminded him.

'And 'tis to Liverpool we're on our way,' put in Mulrooney.

'We play at the Theatre Royal there next week,' said Dempsey. 'I presume you know *The Merchant of Venice*? I play Antonio. Mrs Heller plays Portia, and Mulrooney is Shylock.'

As Dempsey indicated the Irishman, Mulrooney's entire appearance was transformed. His back became bent, his shoulders raised, his eyes narrowed and his mouth twisted. Fixing his eyes first on Jeremy, and then glowering at Dempsey with a look full of hatred and cruelty, he rose slowly from his chair.

'Signor Antonio,' he purred, sidling up to Dempsey, 'many a time and oft in the Rialto you have rated me about my moneys and my nuisances. Still I have borne you with a patient shrug.'

And as he shrugged, he tilted his head to one side, giving Dempsey such a fiendish look that Jeremy involuntarily shrank away.

'For sufferance is the badge of all our tribe,' Mulrooney continued in a whining voice, which suddenly turned to anger as he spat out, '*You call me misbeliever, cut-throat dog...*'

At which Dempsey laughed aloud and broke the tension,

patting the Irishman on the shoulder and declaring, 'Excellent, excellent! How's that for acting, my boy?'

Jeremy was too impressed to reply. He sat with his mouth open, surprised to see Shylock dissolve into Mulrooney again, all in the twinkling of an eye.

'Pooh!' demanded Mrs Heller. 'Why ask a mere boy? What can a boy know about it? If I hadn't been so cold and tired I might have shown him some real acting. Take it from me, young man, until you have seen either myself, or perhaps Sarah Siddons, you cannot imagine what good acting is.'

'But I have already seen you,' said Jeremy.

'Seen me?' asked the actress.

'Indeed, yes. And Mrs Siddons, also.'

'Oh, fie on Mrs Siddons!' snapped Mrs Heller. 'As long as you have seen me, that is all that matters.'

At this point, Mr Bassenthwaite and his serving-maid came in with the various beverages, and the company soon began to unbend.

'Tell me,' said Dempsey. 'What sort of plays are your favourites?'

'Oh! Let me see. I like Shakespeare, and some of Mr Sheridan's.'

'Sheridan's?' asked Dempsey.

'I once took the part of Bob Acres in some private theatricals,' Jeremy told him, eagerly remembering the occasion. 'Some of my father's friends thought I did it excellently.'

'Bob Acres!'

Mulrooney was delighted to hear the name. He had been talking to Miss Matilda, but leaving her, he came across the room, placing his glass on the table as he passed.

'May I introduce you to Sir Lucius O'Trigger,' he said, indicating Mr Cadwallader, 'and, Mr Acres, I'm delighted to embrace you.'

Jeremy felt so embarrassed at being embraced, he could have fled. Then Mulrooney took a step aside and Jeremy was aware of everyone staring at him, expectantly. What did they want? Oh, surely, not the next line? Did they expect him to make good his boast?

But what was the next line?

'*My dear Sir Lucius…*' whispered Dempsey in his ear.

'My dear Sir Lucius,' faltered Jeremy. 'Do you…?'

'I kiss your hand,' prompted Dempsey.

'I kiss your hand,' repeated Jeremy in an artificial voice, bending over the Irishman's wart-covered wrist.

But Mulrooney was carried away by the action of the play.

'Pray, my friend,' he demanded in the character of Sir Lucius. 'What has brought you so suddenly to Bath?'

Ah! At last Jeremy had his bearings. This was the end of the third act. With no hesitation he strode up to the Irishman just as he had seen it done at the theatre.

'Faith!' he declared in a tremendous voice that nearly bowled his hearers over. 'I have followed Cupid's jack-o'-lantern and find myself in a quagmire at last. In short, I have been very ill-used, Sir Lucius. I don't choose to mention names, but look on me as a very ill-used gentleman.'

At which all the company gave the very ill-used gentleman a hearty round of applause. Even Mrs Heller joined in.

'Marvellous!' declared Dempsey. 'Marvellous!'

Jeremy went pink with embarrassment.

'And what a waste of talent!' added Mulrooney, shaking his head sadly.

'It calls for a toast,' said Dempsey.

'Now that's an idea,' declared Mrs Heller. 'I could do with another brandy and water. But spirits are not for you, James Dempsey. If you have to drink, let it be water, or a strong brew of China tea.'

'Nonsense!' laughed the actor. 'This is a time for celebration.'

'Really!' Mrs Heller's voice was serious. 'What about the Old Complaint, James Dempsey?'

A hush fell upon the company.

'Don't forget the Old Complaint,' she repeated solemnly.

Jeremy remembered his father telling him something about Dempsey and the Old Complaint, how it affected the actor's performances, and sometimes made him unable to appear at all. It must be a nasty complaint, for when it afflicted him, the actor's voice became distorted and his gestures vague. Several times it had caused him to be hissed off the stage. At others, the play had been changed and the audience informed that 'Mr Dempsey unfortunately could not appear as he was suffering from an *Old Complaint*'. Jeremy recalled his father remarking that James Dempsey might well have been the greatest actor of his day, had it not been for the Old Complaint.

'Mr Dempsey,' he said, taking hold of the actor's sleeve.

Dempsey had been laughingly refuting Henrietta's fears.

'What is it, my boy?'

'I hope you won't mind my telling you this, sir.'

'Yes?'

'My Uncle Reuben suffers from the 'plexy. It gets him really bad now and again.'

'The *'plexy*?' Dempsey looked puzzled.

'At times he's been quite ill with it,' went on Jeremy. 'But now, it seems, he's found a man to cure it.'

Dempsey's brows contracted.

'Why do you say this?' he asked, and there was a trace of irritability in his voice.

'Well,' Jeremy was aware of the need to tread with care, 'I have heard it said – and Mrs Heller has just reminded me – that you suffer from an Old Complaint…'

Just for a second Dempsey's face betrayed his annoyance. Then he bit his lip and the slight flush of anger died away.

'I'm sorry if I've offended you, sir,' faltered Jeremy.

'No. Not at all. Not a bit of it,' replied the actor. 'What you say is perfectly true. I have suffered from a complaint.'

'Well, my uncle, sir…'

'You say he's found a cure?'

'For the 'plexy, whatever that might be.'

'From some apothecary, I have no doubt?' enquired Dempsey, watching Jeremy with some interest.

'Yes. That's it. An apothecary who is fairly new to Penkley. He sends his boy along with a box of pills about once a week.'

'Send a boy, does he?' asked Dempsey. 'And what's he like, this apothecary? I have met many of them.'

'He's small and sallow, and… he speaks with a sort of Welsh accent.'

'Would you say he spoke like this, hinny?'

'Why, yes!' gasped Jeremy. 'That's Mr Woodrow to the life!'

'And does he smile and wink... like this?'

'Exactly!'

'I've met that man,' said Dempsey. 'An excellent fellow at his trade. One of the cunningest at his business, believe me. But... don't ever mention my name to him, will you, now? We are not – how shall I put it? – the best of friends any more.'

'Yet couldn't he help you... with the Old Complaint?' asked the boy.

'He's tried,' replied the actor. 'But there's only one man who could ever hope to cure it for me.'

'I'm glad to hear that,' said Jeremy. 'I sincerely hope you've been to see him.'

'I have indeed,' was the reply, 'and he's doing all he can.'

Mulrooney was already busying himself with ordering the glasses to be replenished.

'We must certainly drink a toast,' said Dempsey, 'and I'll propose it. I must, however, have my special bottle – for myself and the boy. Oh, there's nothing alarming about my special bottle, Henrietta, I do assure you.'

'Remember the Old Complaint,' she warned him in the voice of a tragedienne. 'Remember we are due to board the coach in an hour's time.'

'Don't let it bother you,' he smiled. 'It is a special vintage of my own. For very special occasions only.'

But the very mention of a special vintage made Mrs Heller uneasy. She spoke sharply to Mulrooney about it as Dempsey slipped out of the room to get the bottle from his luggage. The Irishman made light of the matter, saying, 'James is no fool!' But nevertheless, it was obvious that he was not too happy either, nor were the other members of the company.

Dempsey was back in a moment, and placed two bottles on the table. He was full of high spirit and joked loudly with Mulrooney as he drew the corks.

'Glasses!' he called. 'Ask the landlord for some glasses.'

Turning round, however, he caught sight of Mrs Heller glowering at him.

'Come on, Henrietta,' he urged. 'Smile! Put on a cheerful face.'

He then filled two glasses and handed one to Jeremy.

'Are we all charged?' he enquired. 'Then I give you a toast: to our young friend, Jeremy Blatchford. May he prosper in everything he undertakes. May all his ambitions be realised. May he continue to give delight with his acting as he has delighted us today. And may he always be happy and blessed with good fortune. Ladies and gentlemen, I give you – Jeremy Blatchford.'

Jeremy was so flattered and confused he could do no more than stammer a few words of thanks and then gulp down a mouthful of Dempsey's special vintage. It was indeed a curious brew – like sweetened water with a suggestion of caraway seed.

Dempsey was laughing and joking now, quite unlike the serious man of a few minutes earlier when he had been talking about the apothecary. He drained his glass and refilled it.

'James Dempsey!' warned his guardian angel.

'How delightfully you speak my name,' he returned. 'You make it sound so majestic and awe-inspiring. You have the gift of declamation, Henrietta. You sound words forth like clarion calls. You charge the simplest monosyllable with meaning and drama. You have genius, Henrietta. That's what it is – genius!'

'James Dempsey,' she repeated. 'I asked you not to forget the Old Complaint.'

'What a worry you are!' he cajoled her, filling his glass for the third time. 'As if I am likely to forget the Old Complaint, when so many people have pointed fingers of scorn at me on account of it.'

Jeremy thought he discerned a thickening of the consonants. The words as Dempsey said them were almost 'fingerish of schorn'. As he grew more and more voluble, there was no doubt of it. He refilled his glass again and again, and words tumbled out of him. The more he talked, the less the others did, and there was an increasing look of alarm on all their faces.

Eventually Mulrooney took him by the arm.

'I say... an' it's me, an old friend, that's sayin' it, James,' he began.

'An old friend! Ah, yes, indeed! An old friend you are, too, Michael,' said Dempsey, embracing him. 'An old friend and a good actor. Yes, a great actor, Michael Mulrooney. One of the best.'

He turned, a little unsteadily, to Jeremy.

'I must tell you, Jeremy, my boy,' he said thickly, 'Michael Mulrooney is one of the best, absolutely one of the best.'

As he tried to refill his glass, Mulrooney took the bottle away. Dempsey eyed him severely.

'What are you doing?' he demanded. 'I only wanted a little drink. You know I don't often have a little drinks.'

'Ah, you've had enough, James. To be sure, you have!'

'Now, now!' laughed Dempsey. 'I've hardly had a drop.'

He made a snatch for the bottle.

'No, James, no.'

Dempsey swayed dangerously on his feet and glared at Mulrooney.

'Give – me – that – boll,' he demanded, one word at a time.

There was a frightening silence.

'Give it to him,' ordered Mrs Heller. 'What does it matter? He's done the deed. He's back again where he used to be.'

Mulrooney came forward with the bottle and emptied the contents into Dempsey's unsteady glass.

'That's a good fellow, Mulrooney. I said you were a good fellow.'

It was then that Jeremy felt Mrs Heller plucking at his sleeve.

'Yes, ma'am?'

'I think you had better go home, boy.'

'Yes, ma'am.'

Sadly, he picked up his cap, feeling that everyone in the room, apart from Dempsey, was sad, too.

'Jeremy,' called Dempsey, taking hold of him by the shoulder. 'You can't go home yet.'

'He must go home,' said Mrs Heller sternly.

'Well, if he musht, he musht, I sh'pose,' conceded Dempsey, and released his grip. 'Good luck, my boy,' he added. 'And God bless. God bless.'

Jeremy turned to go, and as he did so, Dempsey winked at him – winked in a very odd way, too, with a nod, just as Josiah Woodrow did.

Jeremy's heart was full, and tears were beginning to well up in his eyes as he bade them all goodbye. What a wonderful afternoon it had been... like a dream. Then, suddenly, the whole house of cards had collapsed.

He walked slowly and sadly homeward. The taste of mild caraway seed was in his mouth. Funny how that special vintage had reacted on Dempsey, yet had not the slightest effect on Jeremy.

But then, with the Old Complaint, anything was possible.

Two: Precursor of fierce events

The short hours of daylight were coming to their end as Jeremy climbed the street to the Gable House, where he lived with his uncle. He knocked on the heavy door and the old housekeeper, Martha, admitted him. In the low, dark room at the rear of the house, Uncle Reuben was seated at table, a large napkin draped over his waistcoat.

'Well, boy?'

Jeremy was not sure what his guardian meant. The question could be an enquiry after his health, a request for information, or a rebuke.

So Jeremy said, 'Good evening, Uncle,' and hoped this would be satisfactory as a reply.

Uncle Reuben took a deep draught from a pewter mug.

'Well?' he asked again, looking his nephew up and down. 'What have you learnt today?'

'Oh!' Jeremy cast his mind back. 'We've been ciphering and working out practical accounts, sir. So many bales of cloth at so much, and so many broom handles at so much else.'

'Broom handles?' queried the mill owner. 'Broom handles? I don't deal in broom handles.'

'It was just to make up the sum, Uncle.'

Uncle Reuben forked mutton and potatoes into his mouth and continued to eye Jeremy up and down.

'What else did tha do?' he enquired.

'A page or two of Caesar's *Gallic Wars*.'

'And what in t' name o' thunder might they be?'

'It's a book about Caesar's wars, how he fought the Gallic tribes, and dug pits, and made fortifications—'

'Is it, now? And what use is all that? I suppose the parson's lad an' thee are goin' out diggin' pits, an' fightin' Gallic tribes, eh?'

'No. But it's a book which teaches us to translate Latin.'

'Translate Latin!' sneered his uncle. 'Fiddle-faddle! Nonsense! Perhaps I'd ha' done better puttin' thee straight into t' counting house. I should ha' known what 'ud 'appen sendin' thee to get learnin' from a parson.'

He chewed away in an angry silence. While he did so, the old serving-woman placed Jeremy's meal on the table.

'And where hast tha been since lessons finished?' demanded Uncle Reuben.

Jeremy hesitated. His uncle would be displeased by the truth, but would soon uncover any attempt at lying.

'Well? Where?' asked his uncle.

'I happened to be passing the Packhorse,' began Jeremy.

'Did you, indeed?'

'And I saw a man I'd seen in London—'

'A man you'd seen in London?' His uncle's eyes narrowed. 'What sort of a man?'

'An actor named James Dempsey. He's very well known.'

'An *actor*?' thundered his uncle. 'Can you only think of actors?'

'I never expected him to come to Penkley, Uncle.'

'No. I don't suppose you did. This is no place for actors. They'll do no good here, and do thee no good either. What was he doing in Penkley, then?'

'Passing through, waiting for the Liverpool coach.'

'Then I hope he's gone with it. And good riddance. What wi' Latin and actors, tha mind'll never get down to the real business of making a living.'

Uncle Reuben drained his mug, wiped his mouth, and threw the napkin onto the table.

'Actors!' he grumbled. 'Actors! At a time like this!'

He rose slowly to his feet and crossed to his chair by the fireside.

'Actors aren't necessary in Penkley,' he said. 'Because we don't deal in make-believe here. We deal in the thing itself.'

He picked up the poker and stirred up the coals.

'Woman!' he yelled. 'Where's that old hag? Bestir thaself, you old Lancashire witch, and fetch some coals in, or 'appen we'll try burnin' thee instead!'

He watched the old woman as she panted into the room, and

added, 'Yet I doubt if we'd get much out o' thee, tha old bone-bag!'

While waiting for her to bring in the scuttle, Uncle Reuben weighed the heavy poker in his hand like a cavalryman feeling the balance of a new sabre. There was a largish black cinder in the grate amidst a host of small glowing pieces. Aiming at this, he first tapped it gently with the tip of the poker, then suddenly hit it so savagely that fragments scattered everywhere. One of them flew back against his top boots and dropped onto the little piece of rug which graced the hearth.

He snatched it up at once and tossed it back, but not before the smell of singeing wool had filled the room.

'I'll smash 'em like that,' he said, deep in his own thoughts. Then he bent down and carefully examined the scorch in the hearthrug.

'Happen there'll be a stronger smell o' burning soon,' he observed. 'Maybe more than a bit of old matting afire.'

He looked up and glared at Jeremy.

'Aye! 'Appen there will. But if there is, I'll fight 'em! I'll outwit 'em! I'll show 'em who's master in Penkley.'

He was so vehement that Jeremy hardly dared to eat lest his uncle should regard eating as a frivolous occupation at such a time. But Jeremy had a boy's appetite, so, while Uncle Reuben was not looking, he took surreptitious bites.

'This is a bad day for Penkley,' declared his uncle. 'It's a bad day for me, too, I'll not deny that. But I'm forced into it.'

Jeremy had raised his mug. At these words he lowered it slowly.

'Why do you say that, Uncle?'

'Why? Because I've closed t' mill. Locked t' gates. Barred t' windows. Let fire out in t' engine house.'

'But... but... why?'

'Because it's no good spinning cotton no one wants to weave. What the good o' paying two or three hundred millhands just to stuff my warehouse full? What's the good o' burning up good coal and wearing out good machinery? Trade's bad. Goods can't be sold. That's the reason, lad.'

The thought of the mill being closed was so appalling that Jeremy could hardly believe it.

'Takes thee feer aback, don't it?' went on his uncle. 'But the decision may be thine some day. What will Mr Tankard the Younger do if that time should arrive?'

Jeremy deeply resented his uncle's attempt to foist the surname of 'Tankard' upon him. But he ignored it and endeavoured to answer the question seriously.

'I suppose in similar circumstances, I'd have to close the mill, just as you've done, Uncle.'

'I suppose tha would,' agreed his uncle bitterly. 'That is, if there's a mill to be closed. If it hasn't been burned to the ground years before.'

'But of course there'll be a mill,' said Jeremy reassuringly.

'That's reet, lad!' said Uncle Reuben, raising his head. 'Of course there'll be a mill! You and I will make sure of it. We'll stand fast, together.'

For the first time since he had met his uncle, Jeremy felt there was a feeling of genuine warmth in his tone. This hard man was almost friendly. He looked across at his nephew, not exactly with tenderness, but with pride.

'They'll hate us for it,' he said. 'They'll hate us. But they're ignorant and stupid, Jeremy, lad. And we'll beat 'em. We'll beat 'em because we're clever. We'll remain masters.'

He was looking at Jeremy defiantly when there was a sudden rat-tat on the street door.

'Woman!' yelled Uncle Reuben. 'Where's that walking carcase?'

'Don't bother her,' volunteered Jeremy. 'I'll go.'

His uncle yelled again, but there was still no response from old Martha.

'All right,' nodded his uncle. 'But take care. Don't unchain t' door until tha sees who'm there.'

Jeremy lit an inch of candle above and took it with him to cast a light along the inky-black passage. When he opened the door a voice said, 'It's thee, is it?'

As Jeremy held the candle above his head, he could make out the figure of the young ruffian who ran errands for the apothecary.

'What do you want?' he asked.

'Mr Woodrow sent me.'

'You've brought my uncle more pills, have you?'

'I might have brought 'em. An' maybe I've not brought 'em,' replied the lad, who seldom gave a straight answer.

'Hurry up,' urged Jeremy impatiently. 'My uncle will be coming out if you don't, and he'll send you about your business, I can warrant you.'

'Oh, so tha can warrant me, canst tha?' scoffed the boy. 'As if I care tuppence for old Tankard! Let him come out if he wants to. Tell me, what does old Tankard do with all these pills I bring him? He'll soon be rattlin', he takes so many!'

The lad thought this an immense joke and laughed coarsely.

'Well, give them to me,' ordered Jeremy impatiently. 'I can't wait here all night.'

'Now, now! Wait a while. Let's see where the box is. 'Appen I've lost it. Where can it be?'

The lad made a pretence of searching through the pockets of his ragged coat.

'Ah! Here it is, after all. Tha wants it, dost tha?'

He held the box up to the light.

'Let me have it,' said Jeremy.

'Heh, heh!' teased the boy. 'Just wait a second.'

Unwisely, Jeremy tried to snatch the box from his grip, which was exactly what the lad was hoping for. He immediately seized Jeremy's wrist.

'Ah, now! Tha can't be patient, can tha?'

He gave Jeremy's arm a twist.

'I'll call my uncle,' gasped Jeremy, wincing with the pain. 'Let go! Let go!'

'Call your uncle!' sneered the lad. 'Go on. Call 'im! I know he's a magistrate, but I ain't afeard o' that. Though I'd better warn thee, little Tankard' (and he dropped his voice to hiss out the warning) 'if tha calls 'im, it'll mean trouble. I have friends, see. And my friends'll stop at nowt. I can tell thee, tha wouldn't enjoy meetin' some o' my friends in a dark lane, or 'ave one of 'em spring on thee as tha passed a doorway…'

He released his grip and flung Jeremy's arm away from him.

'So 'ere… take 'is pills! I 'ope they stick in 'is gullet and kill 'im stone dead. I'd like to see old Tankard stone dead – and thee, too.'

He gave an ugly grin and turned to go.

'Hey!' he called suddenly, checking himself. 'Don't shut the door. What's this on the step?'

He peered down, but although Jeremy followed his gaze he could see nothing.

'Tha doesna believe me, eh? Think I'm larkin' about? Well, listen.'

He aimed a kick at whatever was on the step and there was a hollow sound as if he had kicked a wooden box.

'What is it?' asked Jeremy.

'Don't ask me. I ain't the owner of a big house. People don't leave things for me! Happen it's a brace o' fat poultry, or a big leg o' mutton, or a flitch o' bacon. Not as I knows much about such things. But you rich folk up 'ere don't starve. Not like us'ns down yon.'

Although still highly suspicious of the caller's intentions, especially after his threats, Jeremy opened the door as wide as the chain would permit, and held the candle out at arm's length. The other lad shielded its guttering flame while they both looked down. Sure enough, an old wooden box was on the step, its contents covered with a piece of sacking.

'I wonder what that can be!' gasped Jeremy.

The other lad spat. 'Folk don't send us no boxes,' he declared viciously, giving the box another kick.

'Hold hard!' remonstrated Jeremy. 'You might damage it.'

'So I might,' returned the lad, giving it a further kick before jumping down the steps and running off into the night.

Jeremy unchained the door, set the candle down on a little shelf, and went out to bring the box in. There was hardly any weight to it.

'What hast tha there?' asked his uncle as he carried it into the room.

'I don't know. It was left on the step.'

'On t' step, was it?' growled his uncle, giving it a suspicious look. 'Summat yon old woman's left out, no doubt.'

He struck a blow on the kitchen door.

'Woman!'

Old Martha came shuffling in. She had wrapped a shawl around her shoulders and lifted a fold of it over her head.

'Here's a box left on the step,' said Uncle Reuben accusingly. 'Is it thine?'

'A box? Nay. I've no box. What box dost tha mean?'

'You old blindworm! Canst not see yon box on t' table? Look at it. It's big enough, en't it?'

'It's not mine,' she said shaking her old head, and trying to puzzle out what all the bother was about.

'Bah!' Uncle Reuben gave her a push and sent her tottering against the wall. 'There's more sense in a halfwit. Come on, lad. Let's look at it ourselves. What the good of asking owt of this 'un?'

He pulled aside the sacking, and as he did so a dirty piece of paper fluttered out and fell under the table.

'What was that?' asked Uncle Reuben.

'A note, I think.'

Jeremy went down on hands and knees to pick it up.

'Give it here,' said his uncle, snatching it and holding it under the light.

Jeremy saw his eyes narrow and his mouth tighten.

'Jesters!' growled Uncle Reuben as he turned to the box.

Underneath the sacking was a bundle wrapped in something like an old shirt. Uncle Reuben prodded this with his finger before lifting it out. Old Martha shuffled forward, craning her wrinkled neck to see better.

'Oh, mercy!' she gasped suddenly.

Her cry of horror made Jeremy dart a look at her. The old woman's eyes were shining like a cat's in the candlelight. They were fixed on the bundle.

What could be so terrible about it? It seemed to be just a bundle of clothes, a ragged shirt, a piece of torn blanket, and…

'Oh, no! No!' Jeremy turned away with a gasp.

A small, bare foot hung out of the wrappings and swung to and fro.

Uncle Reuben had seen it too. 'Jokers!' he said hoarsely. 'They're jokers, these people!'

Old Martha held out her arms. 'Give it me,' she implored. 'Give it me, poor thing.'

She took the bundle gently, and uncovered the baby's head.

'Ah! But it's cold! Poor thing! It's cold!'

She took it to the fire and knelt down on the rug, nursing the child to her withered breast.

'It's cold,' she crooned. 'It's dreadful cold!'

'Aye! It's cold!' echoed Uncle Reuben. 'An' cold it'll stay!'

Jeremy was too numbed with shock to make absolute sense of everything that was happening. He was aware of his uncle remaining by the table and reading the note again and again. By the fire, the old woman was fondling the dead child, pathetically unaware that nothing could restore it. But Jeremy's own power to speak or move seemed to have drained away. He could only look from one to the other and wait for the spell to be broken.

Then Uncle Reuben handed him the scrap of paper, muttering, 'I said they were ignorant.'

Jeremy lifted the paper to the light. The message was printed in large, uneven characters.

'THIS IS THY DED. LET THE DED BURY THIR DED.'

Jeremy read it a second time. 'What does it mean?' he asked.

Uncle Reuben was looking down over the old woman's shoulder.

'It means...' he began, and stopped. His brows knitted. He stared into the fire.

After a while he spoke again.

'It means...'

'It's dreadful cold!' crooned old Martha, wrapping the baby more tightly in her shawl.

With an effort, Uncle Reuben jerked himself out of his thoughts.

'Who knows what it means?' he said angrily. 'Hatred! Bloodshed! Disturbances of the peace! It could mean anything!'

He looked at the dead child again.

'But if some folk think I killed yon babbie, they deserve whipping. I never killed no babbie yet. And as for that other babbie as might ha' borne my own name, she'll tell thee how that happened.' He nodded towards old Martha. 'How could we save t' child, when we couldn't save t' mother?'

He turned away. The hard features were working with

emotion. He clenched and unclenched his hands. Jeremy wondered if he would break down completely. And the thought flashed into his mind… The 'plexy! Was this the 'plexy again?

Then he remembered the pills.

'Uncle! I forgot…'

He pulled the tiny pillbox from his jacket pocket.

'What's this?' asked his uncle.

'Your fresh pills. From Mr Woodrow. Do you need them?'

'Eh? Oh, aye! I need them. I need them bad.'

He almost snatched the box from Jeremy's hand, and, as was customary when he received a fresh supply of pills, he took them out into the kitchen. As he took the candle with him, he left Jeremy and the old woman with only the flames of the fire for illumination. But in a moment or two he came back, and Jeremy was relieved to see he was restored to his usual self.

'You!' he said to Martha, prodding her between the shoulder blades.

She took not the least notice.

'Get thee to bed,' he ordered, but she remained nursing the dead child.

Uncle Reuben was about to prod her again, but thought better of it. 'Turned her brain,' he observed, 'what little brain there was.'

He took down his thick overcoat from the peg behind the door.

'I'm going out,' he announced.

This was so unexpected that Jeremy said, 'What? At this time?'

'Aye,' said his uncle. 'At this time. You don't object, do you, Mr Latin Reader?'

He wound a thick scarf round his neck and clapped a low-brimmed hat on his head.

'Where's that stick o' mine? My cudgel?'

He found it in the corner and picked it up, holding it halfway down and giving it a shake or two as if rehearsing an assault on someone's skull.

'Now, boy. Come to the door with me. See that the bolts are home after I've gone. And wait up until I return. When I come, I'll give two knocks, like this…' He knocked with the cudgel on the wall. 'Then another two knocks. Until tha hears the four knocks, don't admit a soul. Understand?'

Jeremy nodded.

'And get that old woman out o' t' way… if tha can.'

'Yes. But what about… the baby?'

'Place it where we found it. I'll make arrangements.'

Without another word, he set out on his errand.

Jeremy listened to his footsteps until they died away, then he returned to the eerie room. For the rest of the evening he sat in a gloomy corner, well away from the old woman by the fireside. As the hours went by, the room grew steadily colder and colder. But there was no movement from old Martha except when she occasionally adjusted the shawl over the child. The fire died down, its glow growing dimmer. From time to time the coals fell in with a rustle.

Then, suddenly, Martha stood up. 'I'll take t' babbie to her,' she announced.

Jeremy started up, for he had begun to doze off.

'Take it where?' he asked.

'I'll show her t' babbie.'

The old woman moved slowly to the door. Jeremy was too much afraid of her weird appearance to try to stop her. She went out into the pitch blackness of the passage.

Something made Jeremy horribly afraid. What should he do? What could he do? A stair creaked. She was going upstairs in the blackness. He crept to the door and listened. She had reached the landing. A door swung open on rusty hinges.

Suddenly old Martha's shrill voice broke the silence.

'She's gone! They've taken her away! She's not here!'

The next moment the poor old woman was coming down the stairs as fast as her tottering old legs would carry her.

'She's gone!' she sobbed. 'They've taken her away!'

She made no protest as Jeremy took the cold bundle from her arms.

'Go to bed, ma'am,' he begged her. 'Go to bed. Please.'

He carried the bundle back into the room, while she remained sitting on the lowest stair, sobbing and moaning. It was such a piteous sound, it chilled Jeremy's blood. But he was too afraid to go back and try and comfort her. She had too much of the aspect of a witch. And the whole house was becoming frightening. The candle was burning low, and the room was full of big moving shadows around the terrible black box on the table. Jeremy sat down again, his nerves taut, while the candle flame leapt up large and crouched down small and blue. Suddenly, unexpectedly…

Knock! Knock!

Jeremy jumped to his feet, quivering with shock.

Knock! Knock! The heavy blows on the street door resounded throughout the house.

Picking up the candleholder with trembling hands, Jeremy groped his way to the door. The old woman had disappeared from the foot of the stairs, and there was no sound inside the house.

'Hurry up, lad!'

He could hear his uncle's voice, but the bolts were rusty and hard to withdraw. His uncle was getting impatient as he struggled with them.

'About time,' he grunted as Jeremy swung the door open and admitted not only his uncle but a small group of men. As they emerged out of the darkness, Jeremy saw that one in their midst walked in an unnatural way. His arms were pinioned behind him.

'Into the end room,' ordered the mill owner.

As the group paused in the passage, Jeremy recognised the man in their midst. It was a man named Barker, an odd-job man who worked occasionally for the parson and was well known to Jeremy and his schoolfellow, Caleb.

The last man to come into the house placed a friendly hand on Jeremy's shoulder.

'You are out of bed very late, my boy.' It was the parson himself.

'Yes, Mr Openshaw. I'm afraid so.'

'Then lock the door and get upstairs immediately.'

'Yes, sir. But tell me, Joss Barker, sir… what has he done? Why is he manacled, sir?'

'It's a matter for the magistrates, my boy – your uncle and me, that is. Now, off to bed with you.'

Jeremy bolted the door again. As soon as the vicar had gone into the parlour, the door of the room was closed. Jeremy could hear chairs being moved and the table legs scraping the floor. They had completely forgotten his existence.

Slowly he climbed the stairs to his little garret room, but it was quite a long time before he fell asleep. The day had been too full and disturbing.

Even his dreams were disturbed, for he had a strange notion that horses were galloping down the road and men shouting under the window. He stirred uneasily and was not at all sure whether he was awake or asleep.

Three: A dish of caraways . . . and then to bed

Meanwhile, at the inn, Mr Bassenthwaite had been having an unhappy evening.

The party in the best sitting room had been very well mannered and orderly. They were due, so the landlord understood, to leave on the five o'clock coach, but shortly after young Tankard had gone, it sounded as if the very devil had got loose among them.

Quite suddenly, they became noisy and argumentative. There was shouting and quarrelling. The voice of the large lady in the voluminous satin gown could be heard quite clearly in the attics. Then somebody began to sing – somebody who was drunk as a lord.

'Not as I've seen many drunken lords,' observed the landlord, 'but that fellow's as drunk as the best.'

Loud though the singing was, it could not drown the arguments.

'Mulrooney!' came the woman's voice. 'It was your duty to have stopped him.'

'To be sure, now how could I stop a man who's made up his mind on it?'

'I'm not to tell you how you could do it,' went on Mrs Heller, raising her voice still more, 'but it should have been done.'

'I'm only the keeper of my own conscience, dear lady,' remonstrated the Irishman.

'Don't "dear lady" me!' retorted Mrs Heller. 'He should have been stopped, and you know it.'

'It's not an easy matter,' interposed one of the others.

'Hold your tongue, Cadwallader. You held it well enough when he went to fetch his bottles.'

'I'm sorry. But he gave us his word, Mrs Heller.'

'*His word!*' Never was so much scorn put into any utterance. '*His word!* And look at him now!'

'Hey-ho, says Antony Rowley!' roared a drunken voice.

'And what are we going to do about it?' asked the lady.

'He'll be sober before morning,' observed Cadwallader, hopefully.

Mrs Heller gave a snort of derision.

'Which morning?' she asked. 'Have you known James Dempsey when the mood's on him?'

'Fortunately, no,' said Cadwallader, meekly.

'Then you have no conception what liquor does to him. But Mulrooney knows! Only he's such an addle-brained Irish bogtrotter he just stood meekly by and let his boon companion get the taste again. Idiot! After all the disasters this… this sponge! this sot!… has heaped upon us in the past. Weren't you at Bristol when he was drunk and fell off the stage? Didn't you ever hear of the time in Dublin when he danced a hornpipe among Banquo's murderers?'

'Whether his mother would let him or no!' the raucous singing rang out. 'Whether his mother would let him or no! Hey-ho! Hey-ho, said Antony Rowley!'

The lyric was accompanied by a vigorous thumping on the table, evidently from the base of a pewter pot.

'Pity he never went for a soldier,' declared Mrs Heller. 'A drunken soldier is one thing. But a drunken actor…'

'Hey!' ventured the drunken Dempsey. 'Henrietta! My love!'

'Your love, indeed!' she shrieked.

'What about a song… together… you an' me… a duet, eh?'

'I'll give you a duet,' she retorted. 'Come near me and I'll duet you on your head!'

'You're a wonderful woman, Henrietta,' continued Dempsey. 'A wonderful woman. A credit to the profession.'

'I wish I could say the same about you.'

'What about that little song we used to sing in the old days, Hen?'

'*Hen!*' Mrs Heller nearly exploded, and there were sounds of violence as if she had struck the offending Dempsey no light blow across the face.

'Playful!' laughed Dempsey. 'Plenty of spirit!'

'I'll show you if I've spirit, James Dempsey,' she said imperiously. 'How dare you call me by that name!'

Unfortunately Mr Bassenthwaite never knew how this interlude ended, for at that moment the evening coach came into the yard, demanding his attention.

'Where's my bonnet?' demanded Mrs Heller. 'Come on, Matilda, don't just sit there like a waxwork. Find my bonnet for me.'

Dempsey had found a new song, and amid all these bustling preparations was singing 'Lilli Burlero'.

Eventually, somehow or other, they emerged from the inn door into the yard, Dempsey hooked up between Mulrooney and Edwards like a wounded man being assisted from a battlefield.

'There are two vacant seats inside,' the landlord informed them. 'The others will have to mount to the roof.'

'I warned you you may find yourself travelling outside, Miss Sharp,' declared Mrs Heller. 'Didn't I say you needed a thicker mantle?'

She held open the door of the coach while Matilda climbed in.

'Perhaps,' she suggested to poor Miss Sharp, 'if you squeeze yourself in between Mr Cadwallader and Mr Edwards and get behind the driver, you'll be shielded from the worst of the wind.'

Indeed, even as they stood there, the wind was beginning to pinch their ears and noses.

'I'd better get inside and shut the door,' said Mrs Heller. 'Poor Matilda's in the draught.'

Cadwallader climbed to the roof, followed by Edwards. It was then Miss Sharp's turn. In doing so, she dropped her muff, and trying to save it, spilled all the contents from her reticule into the mud and horse dung.

'Oh, dear! Oh, dear!' she gasped, looking forlornly down at the scattered curling pins and faded letters.

Mulrooney released his hold of the swaying Dempsey to help retrieve some of these treasures, but as soon as he did so, the drunken actor staggered off back into the inn.

'Now look what you've done!' called Mrs Heller. 'Mulrooney! Go and fetch him!'

Mulrooney tossed Miss Sharp's muff into Cadwallader's hands and went off to recapture the reprobate, who was already warming himself at the chimney side.

'It's warm in here,' argued Dempsey. 'We left a wonderful fire.'

'But the coach, James, me boy! We are due to appear in Liverpool next week.'

'It's too cold for coach travel. Let's have another drink or two.'

'Now listen to your old friend, Michael Mulrooney, James.'

'Ah, yes. My old friend Michael! You've been a good friend, too. I'll always say that, Michael.'

'Then for the sake of our friendship, James, please, please, I beg you to come back on the coach.'

'No, Michael, I'm not in the mood. It's too cold.'

'But we're only going as far as Manchester tonight. You'll have a warm bed in no time.'

'No, no. I'll stay here. Tell Henrietta I'll stay here.'

'Ah, but you can't. You're coming with me, old brother.'

By main strength, Mulrooney managed to drag him back into the yard.

'Are you there, landlord?' he panted. 'Give me a hand with him.'

As requested, Bassenthwaite joined in the struggle.

'Climb up to the roof, James, me boy, and you can have a nice little nap,' urged the Irishman, trying to lift Dempsey's foot onto the step.

But despite all the efforts of Mulrooney, aided by the landlord and the ostler, nothing short of a mechanical hoist could have got Dempsey into his seat. Cold as it was, the three men were soon perspiring.

'Haven't you got him up yet?' asked Mrs Heller, lowering the window again.

They paused from their efforts, supporting the drunken man between them.

'James Dempsey,' she commanded in the most severe tones she could muster, 'I order you to mount this coach at once!'

'Too cold,' said the impenitent actor.

'If you'll pardon me, ma'am,' put in the landlord, 'maybe, if he could be accommodated with the inside passengers…'

'Of course,' agreed Mrs Heller, 'an excellent idea.'

She fixed her eye on the man sitting opposite her. 'No doubt, you sir, would oblige us all in this predicament.'

The man opened his mouth to reply, but not having a suitable rejoinder ready, merely stared at her with his mouth open in amazement. It was left to the little plump woman at his side to speak on his behalf.

'My husband will certainly *not* oblige you,' she declared hotly. 'We've paid for our seats, and we'll stay in them. No. No, Hopkins,' she added, as her husband showed signs of recovering his wits. 'You won't be imposed upon by this female and her drunken friends. You'll stay where you are.'

'This is ridiculous!' snorted Mrs Heller. 'This is an impossible situation!'

'Apart from the delay,' replied the woman, 'it is no concern of mine. And if you are so keen on this...' she indicated Dempsey through the window... 'this gentleman being accommodated, I would suggest you vacate your own place. Though at the same time, I can assure you, neither my husband nor I agree greatly with the company of a drunkard.'

Mrs Heller went scarlet.

'Do you realise who I am?' she demanded. 'Are you seriously suggesting that I, Mrs Henrietta Heller, should endanger my person by sitting outside on a night like this? Everyone knows what a delicate creature I am, especially in the lungs.'

'Then, your daughter, madam.'

'My daughter is the frailest of flowers. Such an experience would be the death of her. I am horrified to hear a Christian person – if you are a Christian person, which I might choose to doubt – make such a heartless suggestion.'

It was the ostler who came up with the solution.

'Seems as if tha'll have to leave him behind,' he said. 'There's nobbut that left.'

'Excellent fellow,' declared Dempsey. 'Leave me behind. Good idea! Much warmer left behind.'

'If you think I'm leaving him behind,' said Mrs Heller, dropping the window hurriedly. 'You must think I've lost my sense! When would I see him again? What would happen when we came to open in Liverpool? Leave him behind? He'd never come out of his drunken stupor.'

'Sure!' said Mulrooney, still holding Dempsey around the

waist. 'But if he won't board the coach, how can we take him with us?'

Mrs Heller stared hard, first at Dempsey and then at Mulrooney. Then she made up her mind.

'Come on, Matilda. He'll have to remain here. There's no avoiding it. But if he stays, so do we.'

'Stay?' asked Matilda pettishly. 'What? In this place?'

'There's the best accommodation here, I can assure thee,' said the landlord, bristling.

'Then get my box out of the boot directly,' ordered Mrs Heller, squeezing herself out of the coach to the great inconvenience of Mr and Mrs Hopkins opposite.

Matilda followed, to the accompaniment of many a 'Well, I never did!' and 'We'll get started sometime, I suppose!' from the other passengers.

'Mulrooney! You'll have to stay as well,' ordered Mrs Heller. 'Cadwallader! Tell the others we'll be following in the morning. But don't tell them why we're delayed.'

She then stood over the guard and ostler, who were sorting out the luggage.

'Mulrooney! Come and get your box and that creature's!'

And so, at last, the coach trundled out of the yard and began its journey.

Mrs Heller and Matilda were accommodated in the large bedroom over the front porch, while Mulrooney and Dempsey had separate little cell-like apartments at the rear, remarkable for their strong smell of horses and provender.

Dempsey insisted on inspecting his room immediately. He at once fell flat on his bed, fully clad even to his hat and mittens, and went fast asleep. Greatly relieved, Mulrooney pulled the counterpane over his companion's inert form and went downstairs to revive his flagging spirits with something hot and strong.

By midnight everyone at the inn had retired to bed, and only the mice in the kitchen and behind the wainscot showed any sign of life.

*

It was still dark when Mrs Heller awoke. She had not spent a very restful night. The bed was cold and hard. There was a dampness about it which augured rheumatism. So she was glad it was morning, and lit the candle with a bad-tempered pleasure.

In the adjoining bed, Matilda was still fast asleep, only her nightcap being visible. Mrs Heller gazed at her and saw she was too comfortable to be allowed to enjoy it.

'Matilda!' she called.

Her daughter stirred irritably.

'Half past seven,' Mrs Heller announced. 'Do stir yourself!'

Matilda lifted a reluctant head, and two half-closed eyes blinked at her mother.

'Get up and ring for the chambermaid,' ordered Mrs Heller.

Matilda grumbled with her face in the pillow, but finally staggered out of bed, yawning and shivering.

Bessie, the maid, answered the summons, and Mrs Heller demanded hot water, a pot of tea, a couple of boiled eggs, toast, and whatever might be available by the way of meat. A leg of mutton would do nicely, or a breast of chicken. She merely wanted a light *petit déjeuner*, not being particularly hungry. Oh, yes, and before Bessie went downstairs, would she be so kind as to knock on Mr Mulrooney's door and ask him to see how Mr Dempsey fared? Their coach was leaving at nine o'clock. There was no time for delay.

Bessie was back in no time with a large can of hot water and the news that Mr Mulrooney was awake and presented his compliments. He would look in at Mr Dempsey as soon as possible. A little later, she returned again with a large tray.

'Ah!' said Mrs Heller, sitting up in bed and rubbing her hands together. 'What have we here?'

She lost no time in discovering for herself, and was in full enjoyment of the meal when there came a discreet knock on the door.

'Matilda! See who that is!'

Her daughter had been compelled to stand to partake of a few crumbs from her mamma's table. She opened the door as bidden.

'Ah! Forgive me if it's disturbin' you I am,' said Mulrooney on the landing.

'Now what is it?' demanded Mrs Heller from her bed.

'Sure, I hope I'm not interrupting you,' said the Irishman.

'You certainly *are* interrupting,' countered the lady.

'I wouldn't like to be addressing you at an inconvenient moment, madam,' ventured Mulrooney.

'Oh, come to the point!' snapped the lady.

'It's Mr Dempsey…'

'Mr Dempsey! Mr Dempsey! Don't tell me he's drunk again!'

'Oh, no. It's not that.'

'Well, if it isn't that, what is it?'

'He's not here.'

Mrs Heller so far forgot herself that she jumped out of bed and presented herself before Mulrooney's startled eyes – curling papers, nightcap, nightgown, all immodestly displayed.

'He's not here?' she repeated.

'That is… he's not in his room,' elaborated Mulrooney.

'Then where is he?'

'Now that,' said the Irishman, 'is the questions itself. Where is he, indeed? He's not in the entire house, and that's for sure.'

Four: Treason lurking in our way

Like Mrs Heller, Jeremy also was glad when the night was over. He dressed and came downstairs. The smell of cooking wafted from the kitchen. It was the same as any other morning.

He pushed open the kitchen door to go through into the yard for a brisk wash under the pump. As usual, Martha was bending over the fire, tending the pans on the gridiron. She turned round as the door creaked.

'Is that thee, Mistress?'

Jeremy stared at her. Had she said, 'Mistress'?

Martha stared back, wiping her hands downwards on her coarse apron. 'What's thar doing?' she demanded angrily. 'Get out! Get away now!'

'But Martha! I have to get washed!'

'Get away, before I put a broom to thee!'

'But Martha—'

'Get out! I've Mistress's breakfast to make. Get away! We don't want boys here.'

She picked up an iron from the fender and advanced with it round the table.

'Martha! Don't you know me?'

'Hold tha clack! Dost want t'wake her? If tha does, I'll dent tha head in. Now, go!'

Jeremy backed to the door, amazed to hear Martha saying so much on one occasion, and frightened to see her so aggressive. There was a strange look in her eyes, a strange working of her mouth which was new and horrible.

Nonplussed, he retreated to the adjoining room, where he noticed the furniture was not in its usual place. The table had been moved to one end and two chairs placed behind it. He also noticed his uncle's coat and hat hanging behind the door. This was most unusual. His uncle was very late abed this morning.

Jeremy looked around for that terrible box which had been on the table, but there was no sign of it. There were numerous muddy footmarks on the stone floor and the air still carried the faint smell of tobacco smoke.

For want of something to do while he waited to see if the old woman would break out of her delusion and bring him something to eat, he carried his usual chair across to the table and sat down. A crumpled ball of paper was on the tabletop. He made a little man of two fingers and set the little man running to and fro, kicking the paper ball in front of him. Eventually the little man kicked the ball off the table and it rolled on to the floor.

Jeremy bent down and retrieved it. Then tiring of the game, he flattened the paper out and smoothed away the creases. It was the note which had come inside the box.

'THIS IS THY DED. LET THE DED BURY THIR DED.'

Another little ball of paper was encased inside the larger ball. It was very thin paper, such as Bibles are sometimes printed on. Jeremy flattened this out also. There was spidery copperplate writing on it which was very difficult to read.

He wondered whether these were a few idle jottings made by his uncle as he had sat and listened to the accusation against Barker, but Jeremy was too sad at heart to care very much. Everything was wrong: Penkley, the actor with the Old Complaint, the mill, the accused odd-job man, the dead child, the mad old woman. Everything was wrong and unhealthy.

Filled with such thoughts, he toyed with the scrap of paper and was about to screw it up again when the name 'Barker' caught his attention. Then the writing did have something to do with the hearing before the two magistrates! He smoothed the paper out more carefully.

'Barker… Jacobin insurrectionist…'

There were other words. Some of them were quite illegible, but he made out the word 'Sedition' and 'Manley, Oakes, Hampson, Harthill, are witnesses' and something like 'Severn' or 'Tavern'.

He wondered whether this might not be the parson's handwriting. But it wasn't. He had seen the parson's during the course of lessons at the vicarage, and it was much firmer and masculine than this. It would be strange if this were his uncle's hand, then. Somehow it hardly seemed to match the mill owner's harsh and uncompromising character.

Whoever had written it, he felt sure his uncle would be displeased if he knew that Jeremy had been trying to decipher it. So he remade the ball and flicked it across the room. Then he fell to wondering what everyone was doing. Why had his uncle lain in bed so late? Certainly he had been busy for much of the night, but this knowledge did not prevent Jeremy from wondering whether his uncle might not be ill. Another attack of the 'plexy, perhaps?

This led to another. Suppose his uncle were indeed ill, where were the pills which had been so effective in restoring him on earlier occasions? Jeremy had no idea that his uncle had placed the pillbox on the high mantelshelf. He therefore dragged one of the chairs across to the fireplace and stood on it to see where the pillbox might be. There, ranged along the chimney breast, were seven boxes, standing in a row like soldiers. He picked one up and shook it. It rattled. He shook another, and it rattled too. One after the other, he picked up each one, and they all rattled as he shook them. They were all evidently full of pills, just as if his uncle had never taken any pills at all. It was very odd.

At this moment the kitchen door was pulled open and old Martha backed through, carrying a wooden serving tray. When she saw Jeremy mounted on the chair by the fireplace, she gave a violent start. The crockery on the tray slid about and collided. The heavy brown teapot tilted and slopped over.

She scowled at Jeremy with a look of rage and hatred.

'Begone!' she screeched. 'Get out, before I take a stick to tha!'

Jeremy stared at her in amazement.

'Get out of this house!' she shrieked. 'Get out of the house!'

Her look and attitude filled Jeremy with horror. He jumped down from the chair and fled into the yard, never pausing to consider that he could easily overpower her if he chose to do so.

'And doan't tha come back!' she called after him. 'Begone where tha belongs!'

Jeremy found it cold in the yard. He was wearing only his shirt and breeches, so the chill air gave him occasion to consider his situation. He therefore merely waited a minute before creeping back to the kitchen door and listening.

When he was satisfied that the old woman had gone upstairs, he went inside again. Quickly he donned his jacket, coat and cap, and then looked about for some food. He was desperately hungry, and it seemed clear he would get nothing from old Martha. So, without losing time, he sawed a very thick slice from the loaf of bread, and lifted the jug of milk to his lips.

As he began to drink there was a terrible cry from within the house. It was followed by a crash and a thud and the sounds of crockery breaking.

'What in damnation's happening?' came Uncle Reuben's angry voice.

Then came the same pitiful wail which Jeremy had heard the night before as old Martha replied, 'She's gone! They've taken her! She's not here no more!'

Trembling with an unknown horror, Jeremy crammed the slice of bread into the pocket of his coat, snatched up the cap he had just laid aside, and ran out of the house, not pausing until he was round the corner and out of sight.

He was halfway across the town when the rain began to fall. It came so suddenly that he was forced to shelter under the lee of a house. He was cowering there, realising it afforded him very little protection when a voice called out:

'Over here, hinny!'

He looked up. Across the way, divided from him by a grey curtain of water, was Woodrow the apothecary, standing in his shop doorway.

'You'll find it a sight drier in here, lad.'

Jeremy darted across the road, splashing through the mire and puddles, and leaped, panting, into the little shop.

'Take your coat off,' said Woodrow, helping him to do so. 'I'll give it a good shake and hang it up for a minute.'

Jeremy thanked him warmly. It was good to be out of the downpour.

'On your way to lessons at the vicarage, I suppose?' asked the apothecary.

Jeremy nodded.

'A good man, the vicar, isn't he now?' said the little man.

'Yes. I like him.'

'A great friend to the poor of the parish.'

'Yes. He certainly is.'

'He's very good to those old women he employs,' went on Mr Woodrow with a little wink. 'Where would they be without him?'

'I don't know,' Jeremy had to confess, remembering that Dempsey had met this same apothecary somewhere, and had observed him closely enough to recall his way of speaking and that odd distinctive way of winking.

'There must be a dozen of those old women, mustn't there?' went on the apothecary.

'At least,' Jeremy agreed, wondering whether the conversation was leading anywhere in particular.

'And some of them are so old, they would starve to death if he didn't let them make free with his larder.'

'But he relies on them to look after him also.'

'No doubt. No doubt. It's a quid pro quo, as the saying goes. You scratch my back, I'll scratch yours.'

'I suppose so.'

'And he throws quite a lot of work in Joss Barker's way, too,' continued Woodrow.

'He did,' said Jeremy.

'Did?' queried the apothecary. 'Don't tell me it's at an end!'

'Well…' Jeremy was at a loss what to say. 'I wouldn't put it that way. Might be, or might not.'

'You know,' said Woodrow. 'When you said "He did", I had a queer feeling, right here in my stomach. Silly of me, no doubt, but I thought you meant to say that Barker was dead.'

'Oh, no!' returned Jeremy. 'He's alive right enough. But with him being arrested—'

'*Arrested!*' Woodrow stared at him in amazement. 'I've heard nothing of this. When did this happen?'

'Last night.'

'Joss Barker arrested! Now that is a surprise! What would a man like Barker be arrested for?'

'I really couldn't say,' said Jeremy, beginning to wonder whether he hadn't said too much already.

'Such an excellent fellow, too,' went on the apothecary. 'See here? He fitted all these shelves up for me, and would only accept a shilling. A friendly chap, too. I've often drunk a pint of ale with him.' He shook his head. 'Old Joss Barker arrested! I can't believe it! Whatever could anyone charge poor old Joss with?'

'Sedition,' said Jeremy, forgetting his resolve to say nothing of importance.

'Sedition!' repeated Woodrow. 'Sedition!' He stared hard at the boy. 'Not sedition!'

'He doesn't watch what he says,' explained Jeremy.

'Now that's something every prudent man ought to do,' said Woodrow. 'Whatever your opinion might be, it's best to keep it to yourself. It wouldn't do for me, if I might cite a case, to go around telling people I'm an atheist, or a republican – not that I'm either, of course. But it's not prudent, is it? After all, when a man's in business, like I am, he has to deal with all sorts – Baptists, freethinkers, Whigs, Tories, the lot. It's no use antagonising them.'

'No, it isn't,' agreed Jeremy. 'And that was Barker's fault.'

'You've probably heard him being indiscreet?'

'Well, yes. I couldn't help it. He ranted so.'

'Not prudent at all, boy.' Woodrow shook his head again.

'I'm sure it can't be. Such plain outspoken things, too.'

'Church and State?'

'Oh, everything. The King, the Government, the aristocracy.'

'No!' Woodrow held up his hand. 'Don't tell me. It's not prudent, boy. Keep it to yourself. Don't tell a soul. I wouldn't, if I were you.'

He winked again in his curious manner, and gave a little nod towards the inner door to intimate to Jeremy that someone was there. When Jeremy turned, he saw that the door was open and the lad who had delivered the pills stood there in his bare feet. His ragged trousers ended at mid-calf. His dirty shirt had no sleeves and hardly any collar.

'This is Sam,' explained Woodrow. 'If he isn't exactly a wild animal, he's very nearly so. He's not as vicious as he used to be. I've tamed him a little.'

Sam padded up to Jeremy as if he were planning to assault him.

'Hast ate yon big goose?' he asked, with a malevolent grin.

'What big goose?' asked Jeremy, backing away slightly.

'That big goose as was on t'step.'

'It wasn't a goose.'

'A fat hare, was it?'

'Never mind.'

'Don't seem as if tha liked it much.'

'Hold your tongue, Sam!' ordered Woodrow.

'Only bein' civil, like tha tells me.'

'He's still rather uncouth,' said Woodrow, turning to Jeremy. 'But take no notice of him.'

He looked out of the window.

'Well, it's not raining so heavily as it was,' he observed. 'Maybe you should make a dash for it now. There's more big clouds coming up.'

Jeremy struggled into his coat again, and made a dash for it, as the apothecary suggested. He arrived at the vicarage just in time to escape another torrential downpour, and went inside, where he found the vicar seated as usual in the parlour.

'Good morning, sir.'

'Good morning, Jeremy.'

They waited a minute or two until Caleb, the vicar's son, with whom Jeremy shared his lessons, arrived. Jeremy was glad to see him. He was looking forward to the opportunity to discuss with his schoolfellow all the strange and rather discouraging things which had happened since last they had met. It was with some surprise, therefore, that he found his greeting to Caleb unanswered, and noticed that the boy was withdrawn and morose.

Throughout the lesson, Caleb held himself aloof, keeping his head buried in his book and never giving Jeremy a glance or any sign of recognition. When the lesson was interrupted by one of the old women who did the household chores putting her shawled head around the door and clicking her fingers at the vicar to gain his attention, Jeremy leaned over to his classmate.

'Aren't you well?' he asked with solicitude.

'Quite well, thank you,' said Caleb, his eyes fixed on his book.

Jeremy bit his lip.

'Then what's the matter?'

'You don't need to ask me what the matter is.'

'I don't need to? Why not?'

'That's a fine thing to say,' sneered Caleb, bitterly. 'As if you didn't know!'

'Didn't know? Know what?'

Caleb looked up now, and stared straight into Jeremy's face.

'About Joss Barker,' he said.

'Barker?'

'Don't pretend, Jeremy. You know what I mean. *Traitor!*'

'Traitor!' Jeremy was taken aback by the suddenness and unexpectedness of this accusation.

'That's what I said. *Traitor! Judas Iscariot!*'

'You don't believe that, Caleb!'

'Oh, but I do! How else would old Tankard – begging your pardon – your uncle know about Joss if you hadn't gone and told him?'

'Told him? Told him what?'

'Oh, you know. About his revolutionary views,' Caleb flung back. 'I've seen you listening to old Joss as he's waxed hot and furious. You've never said a word. But you've listened, and I know you've remembered all he said.'

'Of course I listened to him—'

'Of course you did! And took it all back home with you. Good at memorising speeches, aren't you, Mr Actor?'

'Believe me, I never carried a tale back to anyone. I swear it.'

'Come now,' Caleb rebuked him. 'Don't swear. Isn't your crime black enough without swearing?'

'But honestly, I never, never said a word.'

'Pah!' snorted Caleb.

'But it's true!' protested Jeremy on the verge of tears.

At this point, the vicar returned.

'Now, boys, where were we up to?' he enquired, picking up his book again.

The rest of the lesson was catastrophic. Every bit of Latin grammar seemed to have flown from the heads of both of them. They made such appalling nonsense out of the simplest passages that the cane slapped their knuckles and prodded their backs more often than it had done ever since Jeremy arrived in Penkley.

It seemed that the vicar had reached the limit of his patience when Caleb gave the most fatuous answer of the day. He was on the point of losing his temper altogether and exploding with rage, when the thinnest of the old women who worked in the kitchen suddenly burst in, and without knock or preface, shrieked out, 'Ah! The fat's on fire, Ye Reverence, an' all the chimbley's ablaze!'

Under cover of the resultant confusion, Jeremy slipped unnoticed out of the house, pulling on his coat as he ran, and trying to staunch his tears.

Five: For the rain it raineth . . .

The rain was still slanting down as Jeremy crossed the church-yard, and the cold sting on his face tended to make him take a more sober view of his actions. He realised he had no right to quit his lessons without permission and he would merit a beating if he ventured back. But he had run away now and would have to face it out when the time came.

For the moment, Jeremy had other things to think of. Caleb had called him a traitor, a Judas Iscariot! The injustice of it rankled. Jeremy's sense of honour was outraged. As if anyone, and least of all his schoolfellow, could believe for one moment that he would inform against such a likeable chap as old Joss! It was incredible!

Jeremy paused for a moment or two beneath the lychgate, which afforded some protection from the weather. While he stood there, he took a bite or two from the slice of bread he had been carrying in his pocket, and with his eyes on the vicarage roof, which he could see above the graveyard wall, he wondered why no one had been sent to look for him. Perhaps they were all busy still, trying to put out the blaze in the kitchen.

Then suddenly, he heard the sound of horse's hoofs.

'Hi-yi! Hi-yi! There now!'

The next moment two horses came round the bend of the High Street, then two more, followed by a coach, rattling and swaying. The two leaders did not relish being out in such weather. They shook their heads, champed on their bits, and seemed unwilling to set their faces into the wind blowing down the bleak moorland road ahead. The coachman gave them no chance to rebel, however. He was a determined man, as was apparent from the way he called out, 'Whoa! Whoa, there! Steady now!'

As the coach went past the lychgate, Jeremy glanced up at the passengers cowering on the roof. When his eyes rested on the man sitting behind the driver, he gave a gasp of astonishment and jumped eagerly into the roadway.

'Mr Mulrooney! Mr Mulrooney!'

The Irishman started as he heard his name and looked down.

'And the top of the morning!' he shouted back, grinning and waving his hand.

Jeremy ran along after the coach.

'Mr Mulrooney, sir! Mr Mulrooney!'

'Stay under cover, lad!' the Irishman shouted back. 'It's not the weather for runnin' about in.'

'But Mr Mulrooney! Won't you ask the coachman to stop for a moment?'

'You don't know what you're asking, lad. We're an hour late already.'

'But it's most important,' panted Jeremy, as the coach rumbled over the bridge. 'Please, stop. Please!'

Mulrooney was impressed by the boy's insistence. He spoke to the coachman, who drew the horses to a halt just as Jeremy came running up. Before he could say anything, however, the window had dropped and Mrs Heller was looking out.

'What is it now?' she demanded. Then, seeing Jeremy, she exclaimed, 'What! That boy again! Hasn't he already brought us misfortune enough?'

'He has something important to say to us, Henrietta.'

Mrs Heller eyed Jeremy suspiciously. 'Oh! I see! About James Dempsey, I suppose?'

Jeremy ignored her remark as he had not the slightest idea what it meant. Looking up at the Irishman, he panted, 'Mr Mulrooney, can't you take me up with you?'

'Take you up?' gasped Mulrooney.

'Surely you could take me?' pleaded Jeremy. 'This is a terrible place. I can't go back to my uncle's. And I can't go to the vicarage. Old Martha's out of her mind, and Caleb calls me Judas Iscariot! Oh, please, please, Mr Mulrooney! You must take me! You can't leave me here!'

'Well, this is a pretty how-de-do,' said the Irishman, looking down with a perplexed expression.

'Of course we can't take you!' snapped Mrs Heller. 'Get along home, boy, and don't make yourself a nuisance.'

'I beg your pardon, ma'am,' implored Jeremy, his lips beginning to quiver with disappointment. 'But I'll die if you don't help me.'

'Nonsense!' she retorted. 'Fat, rosy-cheeked boys like you don't die so easily.'

Jeremy besought the Irishman again.

'Believe me, Mr Mulrooney. I'm in terrible trouble.'

Mulrooney gave him a searching look, and pulled at his nose, trying to make up his mind.

'We've halted long enough,' said the coachman gruffly. 'If you've finished your palaver, let's go.'

'Take me up with you,' begged Jeremy. 'Please! Please!' He tried to clamber to the roof.

'Drive on, coachman,' ordered Mrs Heller.

'No, no,' interposed the Irishman. 'It's running the lad over you'll be. Let's take him with us, as he's so determined.'

'Who'll pay the fare?' asked the coachman.

'I'll pay it meself,' said Mulrooney. 'Now, give him a hand, and let's get him into a seat.'

'Any trouble that results, Mulrooney,' Mrs Heller called up as the coachman urged forward his team, 'any trouble or expense whatever, will be entirely upon your shoulders.'

She pulled up her window angrily. The coach lurched on its way, and soon a fold of the hills hid Penkley from sight.

*

Meanwhile, in the town, events were marching on. With the final closing of the mill, anger swelled up in the dingy streets. Tankard's New Mill was like a great flywheel keeping Penkley in motion. Now it was idle, everything was idle. Hope itself seemed to die. There was nothing to do any more. Those who could lay hold of cheap spirits hastened to get fuddled. Fights broke out, which enlivened the boredom, but left behind a deeper sense of insecurity and impending trouble.

What was to be done? There were men in Penkley who, in

happier days, had been small yeomen with their own beasts and poultry. Had they given up their independence for this? They felt as bitter as the hotheads of the community who urged rebellion straightaway, before starvation and colder weather reduced their capabilities. These latter found many a ready listener to their inflammatory talk.

Fortunately, more sober counsel was to be heard. *Be patient*, came the whisper. There was a man named Dickinson who would handle this situation. Leave it to him. Dickinson, the engineer at Tankard's New, was a shrewd man and a born leader. Trust things being placed in his hands.

Nor was Dickinson idle. He had already been to the mill that morning and hammered long and loud on the barred gate. But only a dreary singing had been heard coming from the prentice house. No noise of machinery came from the spinning sheds. The engine house chimney was dead. The great wheel of the engine was still. Not even the mill owner had bothered to go into the premises.

Then Dickinson had walked up and down along the side of the mill, deep in thought. The rain cascaded from the broad brim of his hat to the cape of his blue coat. But he seemed unaware of it.

After a little while he crossed the lane and turned into a narrow alleyway, leading up a steep slope to the High Street. In a few minutes he was in the taproom of the Packhorse.

Flinging his dripping coat over the settle, he called to Bassenthwaite for a pint of strong ale and warmed his hands for a moment at the fire. He then asked for a pen and paper, and seating himself at one of the tables, set himself to compose a memorandum, beginning in large letters: 'WE HEREBY AGREE...'

He had completed this composition and placed it in his inner pocket when the door opened and another dripping figure came hurriedly out of the rain. As the newcomer pulled off his hat and uttered imprecations against the weather, Dickinson discovered him to be Woodrow, the apothecary.

'Is there a better sight in all Penkley than that fire?' asked Woodrow, pulling out a large handkerchief to wipe his face and hair. 'Nothing like a blaze for cheering a man's heart, eh? Except, perhaps, a drop of something strong – or a pretty woman.'

The landlord fetched him a drink, and for a few minutes Dickinson and the apothecary sat in silence, warming themselves by the fire and sipping their beer.

'Someone had just told me that our friend Barker was arrested last night,' said Woodrow at length.

Dickinson nodded. 'I've heard it, too. Taken by stealth, under the cover of darkness.'

'I'm amazed. Such a guileless man, the best of companions. Whatever could they charge such a fellow with?'

'Aye,' Dickinson agreed, shaking his head sadly. 'Old Barker, a man who gave half his arm fighting for his King and country. He might easily have given half his head, too. Yet he's arrested for sedition.'

'Never!'

'Sedition,' repeated Dickinson.

'I can't believe it!' declared the apothecary.

There was a brief silence.

'The truth of the matter is this,' Dickinson went on in an angry tone. 'When old Joss was in ale, he threw discretion to the wind. Out came all his radical opinions. It was "down wi' " this, and "down wi' " that. Not as any of us took much notice, his pals, I mean – Oakes, Harthill, Tommy Hampson. But there's no doubt on it to my mind, Mr Woodrow, that someone informed on him.'

As he heard these words, the apothecary fidgeted and even spilt some of his beer down his chin.

'Informed on him?' he asked, wiping the drips away hurriedly.

'No doubt on it,' said Dickinson.

There was another brief silence, then Dickinson said, 'And I've a very shrewd suspicion who it was.'

'No?' The apothecary looked up. 'Have you?'

Dickinson leaned over the table and lowered his voice.

'When Joss wasn't in the alehouse, where did he spend much of his spare time?'

Woodrow shook his head and looked blank.

'In the vicarage kitchen,' Dickinson informed him. 'And who listened to everything he said there?'

'I wouldn't know.'

'Who goes to the vicarage day to day and takes back to old Tankard all he's heard there? Who's been bred as a sneak and a spy? Who's father was a brave soldier of His Gracious and Glorious Majesty, pledged to support the constitution and put down all radicals?'

The light of understanding dawned in Woodrow's cunning eyes.

'Never!' he gasped, opening those eyes wide.

'Do you think I'm wrong?' asked Dickinson.

'I don't know. But you could certainly be right.'

'I've no proof,' admitted Dickinson. 'But if the landlord were to come into this room now and find you with a knife sticking in your back, would he need proof who had driven it there?'

'No!' gasped Woodrow, moving an inch or two along the bench as if the idea of a knife in his back had caused him some uneasiness.

'Of course, he wouldn't,' said Dickinson. 'Nor do I need proof of what I suspect. It's plain.'

He stood up and began to put on his coat.

'Keep this to yourself,' he warned. 'Not a word to anyone. All ears aren't as innocent as they appear.'

'That's a truth,' agreed the apothecary as he drained his pot.

Dickinson gave him a nod and went out, and as soon as the door had closed behind him, Woodrow laughed to himself and slapped his thigh. Then he noticed that Dickinson had left his stick behind, his famous 'crab stick', marked down its length with feet and inches, and known to everyone in Penkley. Woodrow slid out from behind the table and picked it up. As he looked at it, an idea formed.

Crossing to the window, he stood on tiptoe and peered out between the red curtains. Then he went over to the inner door and listened, trying to make out what Bassenthwaite and Bessie were doing. When he was satisfied that no one would re-enter for a moment, he quickly unbuttoned his coat, thrust the narrow end of the stick down the top of his breeches by his left hip, and clamped the thicker end under his armpit. Buttoning up his coat once again, he leaned carelessly against the mantelshelf.

He was in this posture, his right foot on the fender, when Dickinson came back.

'I left my stick somewhere.'

'Your stick?' asked Woodrow looking surprised.

'I'm sure I had it with me…'

Dickinson looked on the settle and on the floor around. He then bent down to search under the table, but Woodrow remained standing by the fire.

'That's strange,' declared Dickinson. 'I could have sworn I brought it with me. I'm hardly ever without it.'

'You've had a lot on your mind,' said Woodrow. 'All this worry over Joss Barker.'

'I must be growing forgetful,' the engineer conceded, giving a final look around the room. 'I must have left it elsewhere.'

With a perplexed look on his face, he went out once more into the driving rain.

Six: What, dares the slave come hither?

To be awakened by screams and the crash of breaking crockery is not the ideal way to start a morning. Tankard, the mill owner, literally leapt out of bed at the noise, imagining his domain invaded by revolutionaries and throats being cut on his very landing.

'What in damnation's happening?' he roared.

Seizing a chair by the back, he sallied forth to do battle. But on the landing there was nobody but the poor housekeeper, who was sitting amidst the wreckage of the breakfast tray. Steaming tea was dripping from stair to stair, milk and tea leaves were splashed down the wall, sodden bread lay among the fragments of crockery, and butter melted in a pool of tea.

'She's gone!' the poor old woman was moaning. 'They've taken her away!'

Tankard looked through the open doorway opposite. The room was dark and shuttered. The four-poster bed stood gaunt, stripped of its curtains and furnishings. Nothing else was discernible, but he knew everything was deep in dust and festooned with cobwebs.

Angrily, he pulled the door closed.

'You silly ape! Get to your feet!'

She obeyed, whimpering, 'She's gone! She's gone away!'

'Of course she's gone!' he snarled. 'Dead these twenty years! Twenty years! Get that into your stupid head!'

She cowered from him.

'And clean up yon mess,' he ordered. 'You old bone-bag!'

So saying, he returned sulkily to his room, snatched off his nightcap and flung it upon the bed.

'Idiot!' he muttered as he began to dress.

When he came downstairs, old Martha served him in silence. All her strength seemed to have gone, as if it had all been dissipated in the brief upflaring of aggression which had so astounded Jeremy. She seemed frailer, hollower, more bent, more transparent than she had ever been. The mad light which had lit her eyes earlier that morning had now died away.

Tankard ate thoughtfully. The paper ball was still on the table. He too unfolded it and read its contents again. He was about to fling it into the grate when he changed his mind and placed it into his waistcoat pocket instead.

After finishing his meal, he remained sitting and staring pensively at the bare tabletop, following a train of thought through the whorls of the graining and around the brown knots of the wood.

Suddenly there was a crash at the front of the house. Glass splintered and shattered.

'What the devil!'

The mill owner was on his feet in a moment.

'What's the old crone at now?'

As he stamped to the door there was another crash. He flung the door open and stared out. On the floor of the passage pieces of glass were still spinning round. A pebble rolled to a halt at his feet. The fanlight showed the jagged remains of the pane.

'Down with Tankard!' The words rang out over indistinct shouts, and there was the sound of a group of people running away.

The mill owner stared angrily at the damage for a few seconds. Then he went back to his room and slammed the door.

'They'll pay!' he muttered. 'I'll make 'em pay dear!'

He picked up his cudgel. Standing in front of the fireplace, he tapped the head of the cudgel into the palm of his hand for a while as he pondered this latest event. Then, tossing the cudgel into the corner, he left the room and mounted the stairs.

From his bedroom window he looked over the town. Across the rooftops, the rain looked like swirling mist. The drops danced first on one set of roofs and then on another as the wind changed direction. Eventually, the gust lashed the water against the window an inch from his face and completely obscured his view.

The mill owner then crossed the room to a heavy escritoire with two drawers. Unlocking the lower drawer, he pulled it open.

Inside was a short-barrelled pistol and a powder flask. He took them out and loaded the weapon with one of the bullets he found rolling about the bottom of the drawer. Locking the drawer again, and carrying the pistol in his hand, he went downstairs.

With the pistol on the table beside him, he then settled down to read an old copy of a newspaper, oblivious it would seem to the storm without or the whimperings of the old woman in the kitchen within.

Suddenly, there was a loud heavy knock on the front door. Tankard was startled. He dropped his paper, seized his pistol and jumped to his feet. When the knock was repeated, he went cautiously out along the passage. A yard or two from the front door, he stopped and called out, 'Who's there?'

'John Dickinson,' came the reply.

'And what dost tha want?'

'To speak to you.'

'Aye? And what about?'

'I'd explain better if you let me in.'

'Aye. And maybe you would.'

'It's entirely in your interest, Mr Tankard.'

'Is it, now? But I know my interest best.'

'No doubt.'

'And I think it's no interest of thine.'

'I can assure you it is.'

The mill owner considered.

'Are you alone, Dickinson?'

'I am.'

'Make sure th' art, for I'll give thee fair warning, there's a loaded pistol in my hand, and my finger's on t' trigger.'

'I said I'm alone,' returned the engineer, testily. 'And I'm unarmed, too – with not even my stick.'

Tankard went up to the door and withdrew the bolts.

'You see,' said Dickinson. 'I'm alone and unarmed. You can put your pistol down.'

As he admitted into the passage, his boots crunched on the broken glass.

'Tha friends called earlier,' said Tankard, kicking a piece of glass aside.

'No friends of mine,' replied Dickinson, sweeping off his hat, which was dripping with water.

The mill owner gave him a look which betrayed his disbelief and pointed along the passage with his pistol.

'This way.'

Dickinson looked around the bare, ugly room as they entered.

'I thought you would live in more style, Mr Tankard.'

'What do I need with style?' asked the other.

'Then why make money?' smiled the engineer.

'Eh?' Tankard's eyes narrowed. 'Is this all tha came to ask me?'

'In a manner o' speaking, Mr Tankard.'

The mill owner looked at him, trying to size the man up, and not for the first time. He had often stood at Dickinson's elbow and wondered what the fellow was made of. How had he come by his knowledge? What was he? No common type of man, that was plain. He could read and write – not well, nor easily, but sufficiently. He could think, too, and think rapidly, in terms of weights and pressures, of movements and frictions, of balance and strain. He could look at a piece of moving machinery and, after only a minute or two, say with complete confidence, 'It's wrong there!' And he would invariably be correct. Other men could work metal as well as he could; many were better craftsmen; but none had this eye and brain, the quick 'feel' for where a fault lay.

But, Tankard found himself asking, underneath the technical skill, what sort of a fellow was he? Respected by the men. Always 'Mr Dickinson', as if he were a master himself. Yet this respect was a different sort of respect from the respect workers showed to mill owners. It went both ways, was reciprocated. With his own superiors, Dickinson could be extremely civil, but he could speak out plainly when occasion demanded. Somehow he never left Tankard with a comfortable impression.

'A queer manner o' speaking, Dickinson.'

'Aye, you may say so. After all, it's every man to his taste, Mr Tankard. You prefer to live plain, no doubt. If I had thy wealth, though, I'd prefer to live in comfort.'

'Comfort!' sneered Tankard. 'What's comfort?'

'Now, aye, that's a question,' smiled Dickinson, but there was bitterness and anger behind the smile. 'If you can't answer it, who can in this little town?'

'As I know thee, Dickinson,' said the mill owner, placing his pistol on the table near to hand, 'thou art a man o' few words, just as I'm a man o' few words. And those words are plain and to t' point. So? What hast tha come to say?'

'I've two matters on my mind,' said Dickinson. 'The first is nearest my heart, but not in the end the most important.'

'Aye?' asked Tankard roughly. 'And what's that?'

'Joshua Barker,' said the engineer, and as he said the name, the mill owner's face went livid.

'I guessed it. So you question my authority as Justice of the Peace?'

'Not your authority, Mr Tankard, but your methods.'

'Art trying to insult me?' boomed the mill owner.

'I'm not concerned with insulting you.' Dickinson's reply was quiet and incisive. 'My concern is with justice.'

The veins swelled on Tankard's forehead.

'Harken to me,' he said, pushing his face to within a few inches of Dickinson's. 'Dost hold the Bench in contempt, Mr Dickinson? For remember, to talk of justice to a magistrate is to accuse him of injustice. And I don't act alone. I sit with my fellow magistrate, who also happens to be the incumbent of this parish. Dost accuse him of injustice also, Mr Dickinson?' He paused for effect. 'And let me tell thee, if there's a law in this land, and that law's to be upheld, then no magistrate could have failed to commit Joshua Barker on the evidence given.'

'Do you always act on a child's word?' asked Dickinson, coldly.

'A child's word?' Tankard blinked at him. 'What dost tha mean? A child's word?'

'Let it pass,' said the engineer.

'No, no!' protested the other. 'What dost tha mean?'

'I meant your witness.'

'Witness! We needed but one witness! We had witnesses enough in the accused himself. We'll see what the whole Bench think o' the matter when the case is heard.'

'So we shall,' replied Dickinson.

'And if yon is all tha came t' see me about,' said the mill owner, still red and angry, 'I'll bid thee good day.'

'That was my first point, Mr Tankard. I have already alluded to my second.'

'Hast tha? I was not aware of it.'

'When I was speaking of wealth.'

'If tha thinks I've got wealth, tha's a plain fool.'

'You have a mill, Mr Tankard.'

'Oh, aye. I've got a mill. But I've got a mill because I *worked* for it. Get that into tha head. *I worked for it.*'

He paused to let the point sink in.

'There was no mill before I built it,' he continued. 'So if any man wants a mill like mine, he can do as I did. And this applies to thee, Dickinson. If tha wants a mill like mine, tha can build one thaself. And I'll tell thee how it's done – by hard work, and sweat, and thinkin', and plannin'. Then more and more hard work. I didn't inherit my mill, tha knows. My father was a Wensleydale shepherd. When he died, his fortune amounted to five guineas to be divided among six children. Canst tha do a sum like that, Mr Dickinson? If tha can, tha'll know how much I had to start me off. Five guineas among six!'

He held up the five fingers of his right hand and shook them in the engineer's face.

'I can show you sixty,' said Dickinson, 'with not five guineas among the lot. You were lucky with what you had.'

'Oh, no. I wasn't lucky. I was determined. I drove my way forward because I meant to, because that's the sort of man I am. And that's why I own the mill and why I'll continue to own the mill, because I'm the sort o' man who does what he intends to do. And neither heaven nor earth, nor principalities nor powers, nor all the riff-raff of Penkley who come threatening and throwing stones through my windows will shake me.'

With his chin thrust out, Tankard glared at his visitor defiantly. The engineer wet his lips. He was about to reply, but hesitated, and compressed his lips together as though struggling to suppress an ill-considered outburst.

Tankard continued to glare, as if he had made his declaration and challenged the entire world to contradict it. When Dickinson finally spoke, it was in a low subdued voice.

'I hope I'm a reasonable man,' he said, 'and a reasoning man, too, which may be the same thing.'

The mill owner waved his hand impatiently as though dispersing a cloud of smoke. 'Let's be done with the fiddle-faddle,' he muttered. 'It's not like a reasonable man to beat about the bush. Say what's on tha mind, and then be gone about tha business.'

'Let me begin by saying there's no profit from an idle mill.'

'Ah!' scoffed the mill owner. 'So tha's puzzled that out in yon skull o' thine?'

Dickinson flushed. 'Sneer if you like,' he retorted, 'but bear in mind there's folk who believe you close your mill merely to suit your own purpose.'

'What if I do?' demanded Tankard. 'I'll close it for what purpose I like. It's my mill, en't it?'

'You talk just like one o' your own enemies,' said the engineer. 'They say exactly the same.'

'I don't care what they say, or what anyone says,' returned Tankard. 'It's my mill. If I take it into my head to go and set fire to it, there's no one as can stop me. And remember, if circumstances force me, I'm the man who's ready to do exactly that.'

'No doubt your enemies say the same. But if you did set fire to it, Mr Tankard, you wouldn't have a mill, would you?'

The mill owner's lips parted in another sneer.

'Another piece o' wisdom! Your surprise me wi' your profundity, Mr Engineer.'

'Let me put my case in another way,' said Dickinson. 'You depend on the mill for your livelihood. And so do we. Now the mill's closed, no one's getting any wages, and you are getting no profits. Can't you see our interests are the same?'

'Can't I see it!' gasped Tankard. 'Tha stands there and asks me! Haven't I seen this and said this a thousand times! Why come to me? Go to those halfwits who break my windows and jeer at my name and threaten armed violence. Ask them if *they* can see it.'

He gripped the engineer by the lapels of his coat.

'Don't you come preaching to me,' he said threateningly.

'Don't come and ask me to see thy obvious truths. In fact, Mr Dickinson, don't come to me at all!'

Thrusting the engineer away from him, he walked to the fireplace.

'And harken again,' he continued, turning round. 'Those halfwits ought to get on their knees and thank Heaven there's a man like Tankard in this town. I mean that. They ought to get down and thank Heaven for him, for a man who's worked hard and saved money to build them a mill they could work in. Where would they be if it weren't for me? Ask them that? Now that t' mill's closed, maybe they'll find out.'

He gave a bitter shake of the head before continuing.

'But will they? Your folk don't think straight, and because they don't, tha presumes to come and preach to me.'

'I know there's a lot o' twisted thinking by the millhands,' said Dickinson. 'But if they're plain ignorant folk, they're not to be blamed for it. All the more, then, does it behove us – you and me – to think straight for them. And as for my coming to preach to you, that was far from my intention. I came to make a proposition.'

'A proposition!' Tankard feigned deep interest. 'And what is it that tha's proposing? To buy t' mill, no doubt. If so, let's see thy money, Mr Dickinson. If thy price suits, we might talk business.'

'Aye! Laugh at me!' Dickinson snapped back. 'You know I didn't come to buy your mill.'

'Now that's a pity,' lamented the mill owner. 'I could see luxury and comfort ahead o' me.'

'I was thinking of a lease,' said Dickinson, ignoring his mockery. 'Perhaps you would consider letting the mill—'

'*Letting it?*' Tankard was dumbfounded. 'Letting it?' he repeated incredulously.

'I said "letting it",' affirmed Dickinson.

'Ah! You mean the old dog kennel?'

'I mean the mill.'

Tankard laughed loudly. 'A good joke, Dickinson. Let the mill to thee! Ha, ha! What wouldst tha pay the rent wi''? Stones through my window, I suppose?'

'The profits.'

'So tha'd make a profit, wouldst tha?' asked the mill owner, studying the other with an affectation of humorous tolerance. 'Tha must be clever if tha canst make a profit where I can't. Canst find markets where I've failed? Look, man! Use that reason tha's been boasting about. If I can't keep the mill open, how can anyone else?'

'The people of this town have hands to work with,' said Dickinson humbly, 'and you have a mill and its machinery. Put the two together, plus the raw cotton, and we can produce goods. We may have to sell so cheaply that the profits will be negligible, but at least we should be able to make some money somewhere. We could even capture new markets because of our cheapness. At all events, if we tried, it would be better than letting men and machinery rust away doing nothing.'

'I guessed it,' said Tankard. 'Tha's utterly mad. Tha hasn't the first notion of what tha's talking about. Hast ever thought that already there's more yarn been spun than there's buyers for?'

'There must be buyers somewhere. The world has plenty of folk in rags.'

'Aye,' nodded Tankard. 'Then suppose I agree to this wonderful scheme, what recompense would I gain from it?'

'You would receive your rent.'

'My rent!' stormed the mill owner, suddenly losing his temper. 'Receive my rent! While I let thee and thy committee of public safety run riot on my property. Oh, no! If tha thinks I'll ever let another man take over my mill, tha's mistaken. What's mine is mine, and I neither rent nor sell, lease nor loan. And that's final. Don't waste any more of my time.'

'You're being hasty. I haven't fully explained—'

'And there's no need. I don't want to hear.'

'There would be safeguards—'

'I don't want to hear.'

'You refuse to hear?'

'I refuse. Absolutely.'

Dickinson wet his lips again. 'Very well, Mr Tankard. But don't say no one ever offered you a way out of your difficulties.'

'Not my difficulties – *yours*.'

Dickinson ignored this remark. 'No doubt it sounded a

strange impracticable scheme,' he said bitterly. 'No doubt it bristled with problems, and probably would have proved unworkable. But that's quite beside the point. The fact is, Mr Tankard, you wouldn't even listen to it.'

'Because it was arrant nonsense.'

'You refused to discuss it! You damned it without a trial. You laughed at it!' Dickinson's voice rose as he proceeded. 'You sneered at it and brought forward unreasonable objections.'

'*Unreasonable!*' exploded Tankard. 'What could be more unreasonable than all this blither-blather of yours? Lease my mill to thee! Lend thee my raw materials! Bah!'

'I might have known what your answer would have been,' countered Dickinson in the same angry tone. 'You just want power, Mr Tankard. Power to make us, and power to break us.'

'Get out of my house!' roared Tankard, pointing to the door. 'Get out! Get back to your hovel!' He reached out and lifted the pistol off the table.

'*Power!*' shouted Dickinson. 'Power to imprison, to starve, to ruin. That's all you want.'

'Get out! What dost tha think thou art, engine man, coming into my house to insult me?'

'I'll tell you this,' said Dickinson, as with trembling hands he undrew the bolts of the outer door, 'the wrath of honest men is piling up against you. You'll reap the whirlwind, mill owner. So watch out – you and yours. Your blood will be on your own heads. I'm warning you!'

Slapping his sodden hat on his head, he stormed out, stamping through the rain that was still dancing in the roadway.

Seven: A semblance that the very dogs disdained

As soon as Jeremy regained his breath, he began to question Mulrooney. There were several things he was anxious to know. What were Mulrooney and Mrs Heller doing on the coach without the rest of the company, and what had become of Mr Dempsey?

'Ah, well, now,' began Mulrooney. 'A long tale it is, to be sure. But I must tell you the whole of it or you won't be knowing the half of it.'

From this, Jeremy gathered it was not as straightforward a matter as it might be.

'Now it's easy to explain why Mr Dempsey isn't with us,' went on Mulrooney. 'The top of it is... he's gone.'

'Gone? You mean... gone on ahead?'

'In a manner o' speakin'. But only in a manner o' speakin'. The truth is... we've lost him. He's skedaddled.'

'Skedaddled! Whatever do you mean by that?'

'He's run out on us,' said Mulrooney sadly, and recounted at some length all the happenings at the inn after Jeremy had left.

'And he rode off in the middle of the night?' asked Jeremy in astonishment. 'Why do you suppose he did that?'

'Ah, now! Well, now! The fact is... he's done it before.'

'Done it before! How very odd!'

'We were in Bristol once and he failed to appear for the performance.'

'He came back, though?'

'Six months later. With never a word of explanation.'

'You don't suppose he was ill? The Old Complaint?' asked Jeremy with some hesitation.

'That's what people said,' nodded the Irishman. 'But I'm not so sure.'

'What do you think it was then, Mr Mulrooney?'

'Not really knowing, it wouldn't be for me to say – would it, now?'

The Irishman bent his head as a gust of wind blew the rain into their faces.

'But it's my belief,' he went on, when the coach had turned a corner and a shoulder of land afforded them some protection, 'that James disappears for a good reason. He's a shrewd man, so I don't question him.'

'Are you saying you don't believe he was really drunk last night?'

'Now,' cautioned Mulrooney, 'he might have been, and he might not have been. But he gave a powerful performance, I'll say that.'

'I had a glass of wine out of that same bottle,' said Jeremy.

'Ah, yes. Potent stuff, was it?'

Jeremy shook his head. 'More like sugared water – with caraway seed in it.'

'Was it now?' asked Mulrooney with interest. 'Then I'd say nothing about it. I'd keep it entirely to meself. And if our good lady below should mention it, I'd tell her it was real potent stuff, the old potheen itself.'

'Potheen? What's that?'

'Why, that's the mountain dew they distil in Ireland. A couple o' sips o' the old potheen and the leprechauns are dancin' all around ye!'

They rattled along the twisting way, following the contours of the landscape.

'But what's all your trouble?' asked Mulrooney. 'You haven't explained what sent you running after us as if we'd robbed your purse. What's all the trouble about, lad?'

Jeremy told him the story as best as he could. It sounded oddly unreal now, especially the events of last evening, the baby in the box, the terrifying darkness of the room, Uncle Reuben's knocks on the door, and the prisoner being led in. He almost wondered whether he wasn't relating a nightmare.

And as he continued, he began to understand more clearly just what he had done by begging Mulrooney for a ride on the coach. Running away from home was a serious matter. What would his uncle do about it? What retribution would he exact?

Then he wondered what Caleb would think about him. Running away would look to Caleb as proof that Jeremy really was a traitor. If Joss Barker was not in prison entirely because of Jeremy's information, why should Jeremy be afraid of remaining in Penkley? By leaving, Jeremy was denying himself any opportunity to clear his name. His friendship with Caleb would thus be at an end for ever.

Mulrooney noticed his expression.

'Don't look so glum,' he said. 'Things aren't that hopeless yet.'

'They aren't exactly bright,' said Jeremy. 'Whatever made me insist on coming with you? I was panic-stricken, I suppose.'

'Don't worry,' said the Irishman. 'Michael Mulrooney mightn't be the wisest man – his head's too full o' poetry and fancies, but he knows that fate often takes you along the road of its own choosing. Maybe that's what it's done today.'

Jeremy was rather comforted by these words, especially as he reflected that his own head also was full of poetry and fancies. Besides, the die was cast now. A good number of miles already separated him from Penkley and the Gable House.

It was far from being a comfortable journey. The weather was appalling. The wet slowly found its way through his coat and down his neck. He began to shiver with cold, and was very glad indeed when they reached the first posting house.

'Whew!' gasped Mulrooney when they had jumped down and run into the shelter of the parlour. 'What a blessing this is, to be sure! What a relief to escape the weather for a few minutes!'

He looked around to see what hospitality the house afforded. It was a poor place, with the plainest furnishings, and the fire was half-concealed by a ragged pedlar who sat directly in front of it with his hat pulled low over his face and his bag at his feet.

As the other passengers crowded into the room, it was not unreasonable of Mulrooney to ask the man to move aside for a while and let everyone share the warmth. But the pedlar took it as an insult. Without turning round, he continued in his seat, his hands spread in front of the coals.

'Now, to be sure,' declared Mulrooney irritably, 'it's cold, we all are. And I'm sure our fingers are as numb as yours. I'm meaning no discourtesy, askin' you to move a little to the side.'

But the pedlar was not to be mollified. He muttered something which sounded very like a curse, and snatching up his bag with a sudden flash of temper, strode out into the yard without a glance at the company.

'Well!' exclaimed Mrs Heller. 'The impudence! No consideration whatsoever for anyone's comfort but his own!'

She plucked at her daughter's sleeve. 'Come, Matilda! You look positively frozen, my dear! If you're like me, you won't have felt so cold for years!'

Whereupon Mrs Heller occupied the seat the pedlar had just vacated and ordered Matilda to bring a chair to her side. With the two ladies thus ensconced, the rest of the company saw even less of the fire than they had done before.

Mulrooney, however, was now more concerned in obtaining something to fortify his dampened spirits. He ordered a pineapple rum for himself, and half of the best ale for Jeremy. But Jeremy was far more in need of meat than drink. He had eaten practically nothing all day, and was becoming just a little irritable through hunger. While the Irishman talked and laughed, Jeremy felt in his pockets for a few fragments of the bread he had taken from old Martha. He was trying surreptitiously to convey a morsel or two to his mouth when Mulrooney discovered him.

'Well, now!' he declared. 'Don't tell me you're hungry!'

'Not really,' lied Jeremy, feeling that to complain would be tantamount to begging.

'Then what are you nibblin' for?'

'I took this slice of bread with me from home this morning. I thought I ought to eat it before it goes stale.'

'Goes stale?' asked Mulrooney, looking at the sodden crust in Jeremy's hand. 'I can't see bread as wet as that going stale. But you need to nibble something more appetisin', to be sure.'

While Mulrooney went into the kitchen, Jeremy crossed to the window and looked out to see what was happening in the yard.

A fresh team of horses were being backed up against the coach. In a few minutes, everything would be ready for the passengers to resume their seats, and there would be another score of miles to traverse before the next halt – hungry miles, too, if Mulrooney failed to get him anything to eat. Seldom had

Jeremy felt so ravenous. He would have given his boots for a hot suet dumpling or a savoury chop with plenty of crisp fat.

While his fancy lingered on food, his eyes suddenly noticed the pedlar in the doorway of one of the stables. The man was staring across at him, and as their eyes met, Jeremy felt sure he had been under observation ever since he had gone to the window.

'Now,' said Mulrooney, coming up with a plate in his hand. 'How would a real succulent veal pie suit your appetite?'

Jeremy's face lit up.

'Here's a huge wedge for you,' said Mulrooney.

'Thanks!' gasped the boy, and Mulrooney laughed to see the way he took it.

'By the way,' said Jeremy when he had eaten several mouthfuls and was looking to see where he had rested his mug of ale. 'That pedlar fellow is still lurking about.'

'Is he now?' asked Mulrooney, looking idly out of the window. 'He mustn't fancy tramping the roads in this weather, and I can't blame him.'

'See! There he is!' Jeremy pointed across the yard.

'Ah! Sure! A comic of a fellow – his hat's a masterpiece of invention!'

'He's seen you, Mr Mulrooney. Look! He's beckoning to you!'

'The devil he is, too!'

'What does he want?'

'And how should I know? He'll be begging. That's the top of it, to be sure!'

'No. He's making a sign. Look!'

The pedlar was holding up his right forefinger. He then placed the tip of his left forefinger against the tip of it and the left thumb at the base.

'Devil he is!' gasped Mulrooney, looking serious. 'Here! Wait on! I'll see what he wants.'

He buttoned up his coat as he went to the door. Jeremy, watching through the window, saw him run through the rain to where the pedlar waited. Then the two went inside the stable. Only when the passengers were summoned to resume their places did Mulrooney reappear. He was on his own.

'What did he want?' asked Jeremy as he went out to the coach.

'You,' said Mulrooney.

'Me?'

'We'll say goodbye here,' said the Irishman, offering the boy his hand to shake.

'But, Mr Mulrooney!'

'I must climb up. But your way, Jeremy, lies with the pedlar. He's waiting in the stable for you.'

'But—'

'Shake hands, boy. You'll be all right, I promise. Shake hands, and good luck. He's in the stable.'

Jeremy felt a wave of anger as it dawned on him he was deliberately being left behind. He tried to mount the coach, but the Irishman pushed him back.

'No, boy. As I said—'

The coachman cracked his whip.

'Stand clear!' yelled the ostler.

'Mr Mulrooney!' cried Jeremy.

'Goodbye, lad. And good luck!'

Eight: Full of discord and dismay

The rain had died away completely by late afternoon, and Penkley began to shiver again. Old Kinch, the sexton, had just completed his day's labours and, going back to his cottage, passed one by one the familiar headstones of the churchyard.

He had just reached 'Jethro Hannaford, also his wife, Rebecca' when something caught his eye: a movement among the tombstones. He stopped, looked hard where he fancied he had seen something and listened. But the graveyard was as still as a graveyard should be. He remained motionless, watching and listening, but there was nothing to observe.

After a minute he went on slowly down the path. What had it been? The last flutter of a dying bird? A rabbit scurrying away? A rat, more likely. Wearily, he trudged home.

In the vicarage, at about that same time, Caleb was yawning with boredom. Life with a widowed father was lonely, particularly when one's father was as strange and moody as the vicar.

Moreover, by this time, Caleb was sorry for what had happened between himself and Jeremy. He was annoyed that he had spoken as he had done, that he had jumped so easily to conclusions. Dickinson, of course, had led him into it. But Dickinson had never liked Jeremy from the first.

Now everything had gone wrong. Jeremy had run off somewhere, which, brave though it was, would undoubtedly earn him a thrashing. It would be grossly unfair, because it was not really Jeremy's fault at all.

Caleb had had no chance yet to explain things to his father. The vicar had been angry enough over the fire in the kitchen, which had been most unpleasant, filling the entire house with horrible oily smoke. They had spent a good hour fanning fresh air into the rooms and trying to pacify the hysterical old women who acted as housekeepers. When the vicar had discovered that Jeremy had gone away without any by your leave or civility, he had lost his temper completely.

But now, as evening came on, Caleb could hear his father playing his mournful flute. Evidently his temper had now subsided. His flute playing indicated he was in a reflective mood. Caleb knew that if he wished to speak to his father, this was the time.

He crept downstairs. The faint smell of burning fat and fallen soot still lingered. He knocked on his father's door and waited. It was months since he had been inside this private room. Waiting there made him feel how separated he and his father had become.

'Enter!'

His father was wearing a turban of threadbare velvet, the sort of headgear common fifty years earlier in the age of wigs. He also wore a faded coat – a nightgown, as it was called – another relic of the same era. He was sitting in a chair by the fireside, but there was no fire in the grate. At his elbow on a small table was a huge Bible. The edges of its leaves were yellow and wrinkled, and its spine was torn halfway down one side.

On seeing his son, the vicar laid his flute by the side of the Bible and raised himself slightly in his high-backed chair.

'Come in. Come in.'

Caleb did so rather awkwardly, and stood by the little table.

'It's growing dark,' said his father. 'I hadn't noticed.'

But there was still light enough to see each other, so he made no attempt to light the candle.

'Father,' said Caleb. 'I've been thinking, and I realise I've been grossly unjust to Jeremy.'

His father picked up the flute again, spaced his fingers over the holes, and blew a few notes.

'I might have been unjust to Jeremy also,' he said, lowering the instrument. 'But then I've been unjust to so many people. Really, there's very little justice in this world, and very little peace. Justice and peace go together, I suppose. "He shall judge the poor of the people. In his days shall the righteous flourish, and abundance of peace so long as the moon endureth…" '

Caleb cleared his throat.

'Father,' he began again. 'Can I ask you a question?'

The vicar made no reply, but raised the flute to his lips again.

'You went out last night to examine Joshua Barker?'

His father gave no sign that he was listening. He had replaced his fingers over the holes but he was not attempting to play. Taking this as a sign of encouragement, Caleb continued.

'Would you tell me who laid the information?'

'That has nothing to do with you, my son.'

'Father, tell me. Was it Jeremy?'

The vicar put the flute on the table with a sharp tap, and looked in surprise at his son.

'Jeremy?' he repeated.

'Then it wasn't Jeremy?' Caleb exclaimed in relief.

'I have no reason to suppose it was Jeremy,' said his father. 'Jeremy was standing at the door of the house as I went in. And from the look in his eyes – I could see his expression in the faint candlelight – I would say without fear of contradiction, no, it was not Jeremy.'

'How glad I am to hear you say it!'

'I don't understand,' said his father. 'Why are you so concerned? What if it had been Jeremy?'

'I must tell you about things, Father. The trouble is that I tell you so little.'

His father looked sadly into the cold grate.

'Yes, lad. We have grown apart. Though we live under the same roof, we hardly know one another. Why should it be so?'

Caleb suddenly felt extremely sorry for the forlorn man. 'I don't know,' he said helplessly.

'Why should it be so?' repeated the vicar. 'Why can't I be to you a father, and you be to me a son? For you are my son – and your mother's son.'

He put out his hand, but let it fall, not knowing how to show tenderness and affection.

'Listen, Father.' Caleb sank on his knees at the side of the chair. 'Jeremy and I have often heard old Joss speaking his mind very openly. He used to like sitting in the kitchen here and talking.'

'Yes. I've overheard him myself at times.'

'He was not very discreet, you know. But he meant no harm.

It did him good to work off his hatred of the Government in that way – at least, that's what Dickin— That's what people say. He was in the navy, you know. Had a terrible, frightful time – beaten on the head by a press gang, robbed of all his money, imprisoned in a naval tender for five days with hardly anything to eat or drink. Then he was put aboard a man-o'-war and kept below until she was well at sea. You know, Father, you can't expect a man to be treated like that and not be bitter. Besides that, he lost his hand when a Frenchman hacked at him with a cutlass. Can you imagine it, Father? You've no idea what that poor fellow's been through!'

'Terrible! Terrible! Terrible!' repeated the vicar. 'Oh, but war's a terrible thing!'

'Joss Barker is a good man, Father,' said Caleb earnestly. 'And I'm upset about him. That's why I accused Jeremy of betraying him. And that's why Jeremy has run away.'

'Who are we to accuse?' asked the vicar, seeming to retreat into his own thought-world again. 'Who are we to judge? "As I hear, I judge, said the Lord. And my judgement is just, because I seek not mine own will, but the will of the Father which hath sent me." But whose will do we seek in our judgements, and are our judgements just?'

'I'm sure mine wasn't!' said Caleb. 'What shall I do to try and put things right?'

'If I were you, my son, I'd go and find. That's always a good precept: go and find. Seek out.'

But the train of his thoughts led him into another silent private conjecture.

'Shall I go to the Gable House now?' asked Caleb.

'Why not? Go without delay. Friendship is too precious a thing to place in jeopardy. And so is love…'

He sank back deep in thought as Caleb went out of the room and snatched his hat and topcoat from the peg.

Evening was deepening into night. Already the inner rooms of the house were black. As Caleb opened the door into the garden, there was nothing but the last gleam from the west to see by. He crossed the garden to the stile, climbed to the top of the wall and jumped down into the churchyard. As he alighted, a rough voice snarled in his ear.

'At last, then. So, here's for thee, young Tankard!'

A heavy blow caught him across the side of the head, sending him sprawling into the long dead grasses.

'An' here's again!'

Caleb flung his arm up to defend himself and could see a dark shape above him, raining down one blow after another. He tried to rise. Lights danced before his eyes. He could hear his assailant panting as the cudgel swung up and down.

'Hi! You there! Stop! Stop, I say!'

A new voice, at a little distance.

The blows ceased. Caleb lay semi-conscious, vaguely aware that someone was running away. He tried to push against the soggy ground, but fell with his face in the mud.

'Who's there?'

The new voice was coming nearer. Caleb could hear feet squelching through the grass.

'What's this?'

Hands gripped his shoulders. He was twisted over.

'Master Caleb!'

He knew the voice now.

'Kinch! Help me!'

The old man pulled him into a sitting position.

'What happened?' Kinch demanded.

'I don't know. I really don't know. Help me up.'

With the sexton's aid, Caleb struggled to his feet. Tottering to the wall, he leaned there, panting, trying to fight off the dizziness and strange weakness in his legs.

'Can you clamber over the stile, think ye?' enquired the sexton.

Caleb nodded, and Kinch took him by the arm. 'This your stick?' he asked, as his foot struck something.

'No,' said Caleb, looking at the object Kinch had picked up. 'But my hat's somewhere about.'

Kinch found it, and then escorted the boy back to the vicarage.

Mr Openshaw was still in his chair when Kinch pushed open the door of the vicar's den and half-dragged the boy inside. It was too dark to see clearly, but the vicar knew at once something was amiss. He lit the candle hurriedly and helped Caleb into a chair.

'What has happened? Whatever has happened?'

He stared at Caleb's dishevelled state, the bloody marks on his head, the mud on his face and hands, and the sodden stains on his clothing.

'He's been attacked, Your Reverence.'

'Attacked? What? Here? In the churchyard?'

'Just as I got over the stile,' said Caleb.

'Don't bother talking, lad,' his father advised. 'Kinch, hand over that other candle from the bookcase.'

He lit it from the one spluttering on the table and handed it back to the sexton.

'Go into the kitchen, Kinch, and fetch some water. Let's see how badly the boy's hurt.'

When the dirt and blood had been bathed away, it was found that Caleb had suffered two cuts on the scalp and a graze across the temple. The other blows had struck across his back and forearm. When his shirt was off, long weals across his torso showed how savage the blows had been.

'This must be the fellow's stick,' said Kinch, picking up the trophy he had brought in.

As Caleb gingerly rubbed butter into the stinging weals, his father examined the weapon.

'A nasty sort of cudgel,' he observed.

Caleb pushed his long hair out of his eyes and caught sight of what his father was holding.

'You didn't find this stick, did you?' he asked.

'Yon's it, all right,' confirmed the sexton.

Caleb took it from his father's hands. 'But this is Dickinson's stick! He always carries it.'

'Dickinson's?' echoed his father.

'Aye,' said old Kinch. 'So it be! That's John Dickinson's crab stick. I should have recognised it myself, but I didn't look close enough. Yon's John Dickinson's crab stick, without a doubt.'

They exchanged glances.

'Now, you sit down, Caleb,' ordered his father. 'And let's get your shirt back on. You're in no condition to worry your head about anything.'

The boy looked very pale, and his father fetched him a cup of water to sip, wondering whether he should not send down to the alehouse for something rather more stimulating.

'I'll be all right,' Caleb assured him, and sure enough, after five or ten minutes' rest, the colour was seen coming back to his cheeks.

'Did you happen to see whoever attacked you?' asked his father when he judged Caleb was fit to answer questions.

Caleb shook his head. 'Not properly.'

'Did you, Kinch?'

'Not properly neither, Your Reverence. But all evenin' I've had a sort of feelin' about yon graveyard. Somethin' wasn't right, sir. I didn't feel it was right, sir. I had to go back and try to find what it was. And sure enough, I saw someone down there in the shadow of the wall. All black – couldn't see nothing clear. So I hollered out. "Hi!" I shouted, and they ran off down the beck. But I never seed more o' them than a shadow. I never saw Master Caleb even until I nearly walked right onto him.'

The vicar took the stick and looked at it up and down from one end to the other as if all the mystery of the evening's affair could be read upon it. Caleb watched him with alarm, and at last burst out, 'It wasn't Dickinson, Father. I'm sure of it!'

'Of course it wasn't,' replied his father, thoughtfully.

'Eh?' Caleb had not expected this reply. 'Why do you say that?'

'My boy, people act as they ought to act, in a sort of pattern, according to their character. If a strange figure was seen jigging and dancing in the High Street, would you believe it if people accused me of it – or Kinch, for that matter?'

'I can't imagine it would be either of you.'

'Of course not. We aren't the type to dance jigs, are we? Nor is John Dickinson the sort of man who waylays boys and tries to club them insensible.'

'I have better evidence than that, Father.'

'Have you? Then it's most important we should have it.'

'The person who attacked me said something like, "This is for you, Tankard." I heard him plainly, and it wasn't Dickinson's voice.'

'You could swear to that?'

'Certainly.'

'And he said, "This is for you, Tankard"?'

'Some words like that.'

'Yes. Well, you see what it means?' .

'Aye. It's plain enough,' said old Kinch. 'Yon ruffian mistook Master Caleb for Mr Tankard.'

'Or for Jeremy,' put in Caleb. 'Don't forget that most people here think that Jeremy is called Tankard, the same as his uncle. And Jeremy's about my size and build.'

'Good boy! That's a sound point,' said his father warmly.

'Now,' said the vicar after they had pondered for a while on these pieces of evidence, 'how are we to apprehend this criminal?'

'Ah, Your Reverence!' said Kinch regretfully. 'If I'd only come across that graveyard a bit quicker. If I'd only been able to get my hands on him!'

'Don't blame yourself, my friend,' said the vicar kindly. 'I think it was as well he escaped. He might have injured you also, and the end might have been worse than the beginning.'

'Why d'you suppose he left the stick behind?' asked Caleb.

'He must ha' dropped it,' ventured Kinch.

'But deliberately, I'd guess,' said Caleb.

'I think that's another good point,' said his father after a moment's reflection. 'After all, everyone in Penkley knows whose stick this is.'

'Aye,' confirmed Kinch, 'that they do.'

'I agree with Caleb,' the vicar went on. 'It was a deliberate plan to leave that stick. And where something is planned, consequences are expected, and other things will be done to further any plans made. So, as I see it, my friends, we must keep what we know to ourselves and be vigilant and wary. Then, if something happens to confirm our suspicions, we can act.'

After this piece of practical reasoning, the vicar lapsed into his usual reflective mood.

'Then by the grace of God,' he said, 'we shall overcome.' At which his eyes lit up again with practical zeal. 'So I think it prudent, Kinch, that you should take care of this stick until it is needed again. Keep it out of sight, hidden in your cottage. We have too many old women here ever to keep a thing secret for very long.'

The old sexton took the stick as he was bidden and, wishing them goodnight, departed to his own abode.

Left alone with his son, the vicar was greatly concerned over Caleb's comfort. He did all he could to make the boy as easy as possible, but his blundering attempts were pathetic. He was also troubled in his mind. It had come as a shock to realise that someone in his own parish had lain in wait just over the wall with such evil intentions.

'Murder in his heart!' he ejaculated aloud, as he busied himself applying a bandage to Caleb's head.

They talked very little after the sexton had left. Once or twice the vicar was seized with a new idea concerning the assault and said, 'You didn't see anybody at all when you climbed the stile?'

Or, a little later, 'Was the voice a Lancashire voice?'

But after each question he immediately suppressed any reply by adding, 'No, no. It will wait. Don't trouble yourself. Sit quiet. We can discuss it all tomorrow.'

He then thought of sending for Woodrow, remarking of the apothecary, 'A good fellow, I believe. Always willing to help.'

But Caleb had no liking for medicines.

'Just as you wish,' agreed his father. 'Besides, he's a great chatterbox, and we might say more than we would wish. He's also very friendly with John Dickinson, I believe, and it would be well if Dickinson didn't know anything yet. I don't know what his reactions might be.'

Being a great believer in the powers of strong tea, the Reverend Openshaw decided to brew a pot. He went into the kitchen and through the uncurtained window noticed a string of dancing lights moving along by the side of the church. He immediately blew out his candle so that his view would not be impaired by the candle's reflection in the windowpanes. The lights came nearer, dropping lower as the men carrying them turned off the path and descended the sloping ground to the churchyard wall.

'Caleb!' called the vicar.

'Yes, Father?'

'Get you to bed and stay there.'

He continued to watch the men. They had spread out and

seemed to be searching for something in the grass, holding their lanterns low.

Caleb came into the darkened kitchen.

'Did you say, "Go to bed", Father?'

'Yes. But look out there before you go.'

Caleb peered through the dirty panes. 'What are they doing?'

'I suspect they are searching for you, or for someone they believe to be there.'

'But how could they know anyone might be there?'

'Ah! We'll have to find that out. Now – up to your room, and remember, if they come here, I don't want them to know you've been injured.'

'Then I'd better bring the bowl of water out of your study.'

'Yes, do. But don't delay.'

Even as they spoke, a dark shape appeared at the top of the stile.

'Someone's coming,' warned the vicar, as Caleb hurried in with the bowl and soiled towel. 'Upstairs with you, then. Leave it all to me!'

In another moment there came the expected knock at the door. A grating noise followed as it was pushed open, for everyone knew that the door to the vicarage was never bolted.

'Anyone at home?' enquired a harsh voice.

'Is that you, Mr Tankard?' asked the vicar from his chair.

'Aye, it's me. I've come to talk with 'ee.'

'Then come right in, sir. A pleasure to see you. What brings you out on so cold a night?'

The mill owner came into the room and set down his flickering lantern on top of the big Bible. His sharp little eyes looked about enquiringly, noted the empty grate and the vicar's mittens, and rested for a moment on the half-filled cup of water standing on the hearth.

'You think I'm eccentric, sir?' smiled the vicar. 'I speak of the cold, and yet sit here without a fire, drinking water. The trouble is, I get engrossed.'

'That's your business,' said Tankard. 'Every man can do what he likes. If you choose to freeze, go and freeze. Don't apologise to me.'

'You've something on your mind,' observed the vicar.

'Aye, that I have! The boy—'

'The boy? Which boy?'

'Which boy! My boy, of course. He hasn't come home.'

'Jeremy not come home?' The vicar sat up sharply and stared at his visitor. 'But he left here hours ago.'

'Did he? Well, he's not come home. I can't find him anywhere.'

'But he left here halfway through the morning. Before lessons were finished.'

'Before lessons were finished?' enquired the mill owner. 'Why was that?'

'He had some altercation with Caleb.'

'Oh, did he? Did he now? And you allowed him to leave?'

'Not at all. He left without asking. It so happened that one of the women—'

'I don't want to know about the women, Vicar. I want to know about the boy.'

'He left here shortly before midday. That's all I know.'

'Where did he go?'

'I really can't say.'

'But, man, you were responsible for him!'

'I agree. But he left without my knowledge or permission.'

Tankard glared in silence into the vicar's bland eyes, and after a moment he asked, 'You didn't see him in the churchyard tonight?'

'Who?'

'My boy, Jeremy, of course.'

'No, I didn't.'

'You didn't see that man Dickinson?'

'No.'

'Have you seen Dickinson at all?'

'He was here this morning.'

'What for?'

'A talk.'

'About last night's affair?'

'Yes.'

'What mood was he in?'

'Quietly angry, I would say.'

'Quietly? Not violently?'

'No. Certainly not violently.'

The mill owner picked up his lantern and without another word went out of the room and thence into the garden. The vicar could hear him shouting to the men in the churchyard. A minute later he was back.

'Tha didn't notice anything suspicious tonight?' he enquired.

'Suspicious?'

'Any raised voices? Sounds of a struggle? Cries for help?'

'No.'

'You are sure?'

'Perfectly sure.'

'Has anyone else been with 'ee in t' house?'

'Caleb.'

'Where's he? I'll ask him.'

'He's gone to bed. But he was here talking to me until a short while ago.'

'What dost tha mean by a short while ago?'

'Just ten minutes ago. Shortly before you knocked.'

Tankard considered the matter. 'So he heard nowt either?'

'I'm sure he didn't.'

'Then I won't disturb him. But don't tha go to bed yet awhile. I might have need of thee.'

The vicar followed him out. His men were standing in a group by the main door.

'Found anything at all?' Tankard asked them.

'Nothing, Mr Tankard.'

'No footmarks in the mud?'

'A hundred or more. There's bin so many folk o'er yon stile there's no sortin' 'em out.'

'You didn't find his stick, then?'

'Not a trace of it.'

'Now,' grumbled Tankard, holding his chin. 'I wonder…' He thought for a moment.

'Right!' he commanded, swinging his lantern forward. 'Come with me.'

The little party trooped across the garden and went over the stile one by one. As the wind was very raw indeed, the vicar came back to warm himself by the remains of the kitchen fire.

Once the men and their lanterns had vanished from view, Caleb was too inquisitive to remain in his bedroom. So, despite his throbbing head, he returned downstairs and asked his father what had gone on.

'But how did Mr Tankard know about the stick?' he asked, when his father had finished relating his conversation with the mill owner.

'And how did he know about Joshua Barker?' asked his father by the way of reply.

Caleb stared at him, realising the significance of the question.

'And I thought that Jeremy had been the informer.'

'Jeremy was a logical possibility,' said the vicar. 'It would also be logical to suggest he might have made this attack upon you. But it shows we shouldn't trust logic alone.'

'I'm glad to know I was wrong,' said Caleb. Then, after a pause he asked, 'What do you suppose Mr Tankard's doing now?'

'I don't know. But we'll probably find out very soon.'

Less than half an hour later, there was another knocking on the door. Caleb managed to slip upstairs just before the mill owner re-entered, followed by his five men. In between two of them was John Dickinson.

'I am here as accuser,' said Tankard, when they had crowded into the vicar's private room and the lantern was again standing on top of the Bible. 'It's not justice for a man to decide his own case. So tha'll be sole magistrate, Vicar.'

The vicar took his customary seat and looked around the circle of faces.

'Am I charged with some violent crime,' asked Dickinson, 'that you come out with lamps and staves to take me like a thief?' At this the vicar raised his eyes again to look into the man's face. 'If not, why am I forced here?'

'You are charged with assault—'

'You can't charge me with assault. I haven't assaulted a living soul!'

'Watch your words!' snapped Tankard. 'Or am I to suppose you have assaulted a dead soul… or a departed soul, should I say?'

'I have assaulted nobody.'

'I am charging thee with assault in the legal meaning of the term. Not assault and battery. Merely assault: the threat of causing bodily harm.'

'I have never threatened bodily harm.'

'I accuse thee of threatening harm not only to myself personally, but to my ward, Jeremy Tankard.'

'Is this true, Mr Dickinson?' asked the vicar.

'Certainly not! I've made no threat of any sort.'

'Not this morning, when tha came to my house?' asked Tankard.

'Certainly not! I went to the Gable House to put a proposition to you, and you refused to listen.'

'I told thee the whole thing was idiotic. Then tha threatened me.'

'Mr Openshaw, sir,' appealed Dickinson. 'This is ludicrous.'

'Dost deny it?' asked Tankard, his temper rising.

'Of course I do!' retorted the engineer, turning angrily to his accuser. 'But I admit warning thee of the consequences of refusing to listen to me.'

'Ho, ho!' crowed Tankard. 'So a threat becomes a warning, eh? This is a very fine-drawn distinction, isn't it?'

'I think, Mr Dickinson,' said the vicar, 'you'd better try and recall exactly what you said.'

'I warned him about the consequences. I made it quite plain, I think, Vicar. I said unless something was done to relieve the misery in this town, there'd be troubles. It doesn't take an Old Testament prophet, Mr Openshaw, to see that far ahead.'

'Bah!' snorted the mill owner. 'Tha threatened me in direct terms. "You and yours", tha said.'

'True, I possibly did,' confessed Dickinson. 'After all, isn't the one who has sown the wind the most likely to reap the whirlwind?'

'Don't try and alter thy meaning,' snarled Tankard. 'Tha knows what tha meant. Tha meant me and my boy. And tha's attacked the boy first.'

'Attacked the boy!'

'Look, man,' Tankard went on in the same ugly tone. 'Let's

put aside our legal pretences. I may only charge thee with assault, but I know much more. Where's the boy? What has tha done with him?'

'What have I done with him?' repeated the engineer.

'Yes, sir!' yelled Tankard, exasperated. 'What hast tha done wi' him?'

'I've done nothing! And how should I know what's become of him? I've been home all evening.'

'Hast tha, now?' mocked Tankard.

'My wife can swear to it.'

Tankard's lips curled in a cynical smile. 'No doubt she would swear to anything,' he observed, and then, trying to assume a less aggressive tone, said, 'See, Dickinson, I have reason to believe tha weren't at home at all.'

Dickinson blinked at him. There was something sinister in the way the words were said. 'If that's what you've been told,' he replied, 'it's a lie.'

'Tha were here,' said Tankard, 'in the churchyard!'

'I certainly was not.'

'Oh, but tha were! I have witnesses.'

'Then where are they?' demanded Dickinson, looking about.

'They are not required on this occasion,' replied Tankard blandly. 'I'll produce them when tha's charged wi' a graver offence. In my opinion, tha's an arch-liar, Dickinson, and very probably a murderer.'

'*A murderer!*'

'A murderer!' thundered Tankard, suddenly smiting the table with his fist. 'Come! Where's my boy? What hast tha done with him? If he's dead, where's his body?'

'I swear by all that's holy—' began Dickinson.

'Do not blaspheme!' shouted the mill owner.

'I'm not blaspheming!'

'Let's have the truth.'

'I know nothing about the matter, and that is the truth.'

Tankard turned to the vicar. 'We are getting nowhere. Tha must commit this man.'

'With all due respect to you, Mr Tankard, but I don't see—' began the vicar.

'You must see you must commit him,' insisted the other.

'I can't. The case isn't proved.'

'The case isn't proved?' repeated Tankard, his face going a deep red, and the veins standing out, purple, on his forehead. 'Not proved? When this man has threatened, lied, assaulted my boy, desecrated holy ground and committed blasphemy! And tha won't commit him? Art thou a justice o' t' peace, or what art tha?'

'I have weighed what little evidence you have put forward.'

'I've enough evidence to hang him,' declared Tankard. 'And if so much as a hair of that boy's head has been harmed, hang him I shall!'

'You have not presented any evidence to me,' insisted the vicar, 'and therefore, as the examining magistrate, I must dismiss the case.'

Dickinson had been standing with both hands holding his hat in front of him. Now he slammed the hat on to his head, and without a word turned round and pushed past the men who stood before the door. No one stopped him.

The mill owner remained where he stood, staring angrily at the vicar.

'Dost realise,' he said, 'that yon man has in all probability slain my boy... my heir?'

He took up his lantern, cast a withering look at his fellow magistrate, and motioned his men to lead the way out of the house.

Nine: No news so bad abroad as this at home

From the first hours of Sunday morning, snow had whirled down upon Penkley. By daybreak it had blocked the roads and lodged in a thick crust on Tankard's New Mill, undisturbed by any pulsations from the great engine. It covered the yard. The huge pile of coal had grown bigger and turned white. The unopened bales standing under an open shelter looked like masses of raw cotton, straight from America.

The snow had effaced all the previous day's imprints. No footprints led to the stile across the churchyard wall. There was no trace of muddy wheel marks in the road or across the bridge. In the inn yard, no one would have known from any visible signs that a poor pedlar had ridden in late on the previous evening.

People viewed the snow with differing emotions. Reuben Tankard, tired of rereading a little scrap of paper out of his waistcoat pocket and glowering with savage hatred at the pillboxes on the mantelshelf, looked across the gleaming landscape and tried to conjecture where his nephew might be lying.

John Dickinson hardly noticed that snow had fallen. He was so involved in his own thoughts that he made no reply when his wife had cause to mention it. But to Woodrow the apothecary it was a matter of satisfaction. He smiled as he stood outside his shop, swinging his arms vigorously across his body and stamping his feet to warm them. Then he went inside again, slammed his door shut, put the bar across and brought ink and paper on to the counter. He was busily writing when the inner door opened and Sam, tousle-haired and bleary-eyed, appeared.

'En't it cold!' complained Sam.

'What do you want?' demanded Woodrow angrily, putting his arm over the half-page he had written.

'Ah! But tha knows what I wants!'

'Get back to your kennel or I'll take my stick across your back.'

The threat had no effect. On the contrary, Sam chuckled.

'Tha wouldn't take a stick to me, Mr Woodrow. Tha knows better.'

Woodrow gave him a suspicious look. 'What have you come for?' he asked.

'Tha said tha's pay me a shilling.'

'I will. You'll get it.'

'Aye, I'll get it, Mr Woodrow. And then there's thruppence for taking the pills.'

'You'll get that, too. Now go back to the kitchen. I'm busy.'

'I want more than one and thruppence, Mr Woodrow.'

'What do you mean?'

'It's worth more than one and thruppence.'

Woodrow put down his pen and swung round on the stool. He looked coldly at the ragged boy. His eyes narrowed and held the boy's gaze. The smile faded from Sam's face.

'Have you ever seen a man hanged?' asked the apothecary in a level, icy voice. 'I've seen them. By the cartload. Not only men and women, but boys – like you. All standing in a row with a halter round their necks. Then – drop! And they dance for a minute. Then they are quite still.'

'Tha can't harm me,' said Sam defiantly. 'I'd tell.'

'You'd tell!' scoffed Woodrow. 'Shall I enlighten you? I have friends in high places. In the very heart of London, among the King's own ministers. You'd tell! You! A single word from me would send you to the gallows tomorrow. Go back to your kennel, boy, and thank your stars I've let you live this long.'

Sam stood staring at him, his mouth open, until gradually he became convinced of the truth of Woodrow's statements.

'Give me my money,' he then demanded, sulkily.

The apothecary felt in his pocket, found a shilling and tossed it to him.

'Be a sensible boy, Sam. There may be more shillings yet.'

Sam bit the coin and rubbed it on his sleeve. With a surly look at his employer, he slunk back into the kitchen.

*

From the vicarage windows, the vicar viewed the snow with a feeling of awe and reverence. At first it reminded him of happier times, but then morbid thoughts succeeded the pleasant ones. They might have held him in thrall, but there were things to be done. First he went to see how Caleb was and found him little the worse for his adventure. The bruises showed plainly where he had been struck, but the wounds on his head were not so serious as they had seemed.

'Will you be able to attend church?' asked the vicar.

Caleb felt his head gingerly. 'I think so.'

'It is important that you do,' said his father. 'I know that our concealment of what actually happened last night may not seem very logical – I might even be accused of improper conduct – but I am sure it has already been justified. We now know beyond doubt that someone planned this assault to incriminate Dickinson.'

'We also know that Mr Tankard has a secret informant,' added Caleb.

'Yes, indeed,' agreed his father. 'And there may be more to learn. So let us preserve our secret at all costs. Before you go to church, I'll take care to arrange you hair to hide those marks. And if anyone asks about the scar on your temple, shall we pretend you fell downstairs – and make a joke of it?'

They said no more, for at that moment the appointed servitor for the day made her snivelling entrance with the breakfast tray. She was an incredibly dirty woman, with matted grey hair and a black dress so greasy that it almost shone. The meal looked and smelled as unsavoury as its bearer.

'For what we are about to receive,' said the vicar, reverently placing his hands together, closing his eyes, and speaking with all sincerity, 'may the Lord make us truly thankful.'

Despite the harsh weather, the congregation that morning was in no way diminished. From the moment that old Kinch began tugging at his bell rope and the cracked clang of the old bell rang out over the frozen town, people came up the steps into the porch. Once or twice it was quite crowded as worshippers shook the snow from their apparel and kicked compressed lumps from their heels. Before long, the flagged floor was a muddy pool out of which wet footmarks proceeded in disorderly trails to the pews.

The mill apprentices came in a body under the eagle eye of their master. Not one of them had been left behind to clean the machinery, although perhaps it was the one day of the year when the task would have been welcome. But no, they were all marshalled into the cold and paraded through the snow. The injunction delivered at their baptisms that they should 'hear sermons' was being strictly observed, however insincerely it might have been gabbled off in the destitute London parishes where they had entered the Christian fold.

Bessie was sent along from the Packhorse. At a little distance behind her came the pedlar who had arrived the night before. Little wisps of straw clung to his long coat and ancient tricorn hat, evidence of his having spent the night in the stable loft.

Of the townspeople, there were twice as many as usual – not just the petty shopkeepers who occupied rateable hereditaments and prided themselves on being churchwardens and vestrymen, but millhands who had long since given up any belief in religion, or anything else. There was many a face in church that morning upon which the parson had never looked before.

John Dickinson came, as he always did, but today he was more thoughtful than usual, and he was always a thoughtful man. He made his way down the lane from his cottage, his brow furrowed, his mind occupied with his own scheme. Then, as he neared the lychgate, he spied the apothecary ahead of him.

'Hold on!' he called.

Woodrow stopped immediately, almost as if he had been struck. Then he turned. There was incredulity on his face. His eyes goggled. His mouth was open in surprise.

Dickinson was too engrossed in plodding through the thick snow to notice the other's expression.

'Wait a minute, if you please,' he called.

By the time Dickinson had reached the apothecary, Woodrow was his usual affable self.

'Good morning, Mr Dickinson. How's the world with you?'

Dickinson was out of breath. He stood by the gatepost to recover.

'Things are getting out of hand,' he said at length. 'I can't explain everything just now. But the time's drawing ripe.'

'Ripe? What do you mean?'

'What I hinted at yesterday. Informers. Plots. Conspiracies.'

They looked at each other. Dickinson, with his back to the gate, faced down the High Street. Woodrow stood looking into the churchyard.

'Why? What's new?' he asked.

'I'll tell you later. We'll meet tonight.'

'Who? You and I?'

'No. All of us. The council of the Association.'

'Good. It's about time.'

Dickinson glanced up and down. Other huddled figures were coming towards them.

'We mustn't be seen talking. Go into church ahead of me. I'll arrange to give the signal to our colleagues.'

'They'll be heartened. All Penkley will be heartened.'

'We'll see.'

One after the other, they went into church. As Dickinson went down the aisle to his pew, Caleb passed him.

'When all thy mercies,' said Dickinson without moving his lips.

Caleb gave the tiniest of nods and moved on.

Not everyone coming into church was so discreet. Chatter ran high among those thronging the porch, and men twisted round in the pews to converse loudly with their neighbours.

'Hast heard about young Tankard?'

'Aye. Is't reet, then?'

'Nobody knows owt for sure.'

'Missing, they say.'

'Seems Old Tankard's had men everywhere. All round t' meadows and beck-side. All night they've been out.'

'But I heard they'd found him.'

'Found him? Nay! I've not heard that!'

'Aye. They've found him. Bit with his head staved in. Clubbed to death.'

'Nay!'

'All rumour it is! There's nowt in it.'

'Barney 'ere says they found Tankard wi' his head stove in.'

'They never did! They found nowt.'

'They was down here in the churchyard lookin' for him.'

'Aye, reet enough, they were. But found nowt. Will Turner was wi' 'em, and he told me hisself.'

'Where's the lad gone, then?'

'Who cares? Who's worried about what's happened to t' mill owner's lad? We've lads of our own to worry o'er.'

'Maybe by now he's at home.'

'Aye. Coddled wi' a dram o' brandy to keep t' chill out.'

'Aye. Nowt's too good for t' mill owner's lad.'

The pedlar, who had sat at the back, only heard a few of these remarks clearly, but from the way he inclined his head to listen, he obviously found them of interest.

The apothecary listened to them all with even greater interest, but refrained from entering the conversation. Only when he was directly addressed by the man sitting next to him did he make any comment.

'Hast thou heard about all this, Mr Woodrow?'

'Not a word.'

'They didn't call on thee, then?'

'No. And I was indoors all evening.'

'They didn't need thy services, then?'

'Evidently not.'

Before the apothecary could learn more, the vicar came in from the vestry and the service began.

The reflection of the snow striking upwards through the windows made the church strangely bright. Even the corners of the dark chancel were illuminated, and the old beams in the roof shone as they seldom did, even on a summer's day. But this was not the only thing which made this particular Sunday exceptional. There was a strange feeling in the air, originating perhaps in the unwanted chatter beforehand, but persisting even when the chatter had ceased, even indeed when the preliminary coughs and throat-clearing ceased and the opening hymn was announced.

> 'When all thy mercies, O my God,
> My rising soul surveys,
> Transported with the view, I'm lost
> In wonder, love, and praise.'

The words seemed to electrify the congregation. There was a curious feeling of urgency. Men exchanged glances with their neighbours. Even those who looked stolidly at their hymnals seemed to be hiding their true feelings. Then, when the singing began, it was quite unexpected in its volume, so different from the congregation's usual dirge-like chant. It surged upwards, full-throated, enthusiastic. The rafters rang. Everyone joined in. The old women added their squawks to the deep basses of the men. The apprentices piped up with the few words they knew. One of them even pretended he could read the hymn book.

This changed quality came as the greatest surprise to the minister. He pushed his spectacles down his nose and peered over the top of them to try to discover what had transformed his congregation. He looked at the organist for some sort of explanation, but that elderly man was too busy rocking to and fro on his stool to bother about the singing. That was not his department.

It came as a surprise to Caleb, also. He felt his scalp tingling – not with the pain of his injury, but with emotion. This was the hymn he had waited for. It brought elation to his spirit. The time was at hand. His rising soul surveyed not only the reflection of the snow, but a new brightness shining in the windows of the world.

But if the parson noted a changed congregation, Caleb in particular noted a changed parson. He was not the usual bumbler, muttering the prayers in a half-audible voice. He was transformed. He gave the familiar words of the Prayer Book new meanings. He laid great emphasis on certain phrases, endowing them with a new vitality. When he recited the collect of the day (it was the third Sunday in Advent), he prayed earnestly for the turning of 'the hearts of the disobedient'. The intensity of his fervour was visible in the way he screwed up his eyes and clenched his hands together as he knelt.

Yet, if he was thinking of others, he was also thinking of himself. As he read the lesson, he seemed to forget the congregation. Judging from the way he obviously thought out the meaning of each word he read, he might have been in his study.

'Therefore judge nothing before the time, until the Lord

come, who both will bring to light the hidden things of darkness, and will make manifest the counsels of the heart… Judge nothing before the time,' he repeated. 'Judge nothing.'

Then, after a frowning look at the open page, he picked out the other phrase. 'Bring to light the hidden things of darkness.'

He pondered this, pushing out one side of his cheek with his tongue. Then suddenly he remembered he was in the midst of a service and hurriedly completed the appointed passage.

The service was long, combining Morning Prayer and Holy Communion, and including a lengthy sermon. It was wearying to Caleb. His bones soon began to ache through sitting on the hard pew. The cold came up through the stone floor, and the smell of mildew grew more sickening. He shuddered. Thank Heaven it would be Christmas soon!

The sermon eventually came to its conclusion. The congregation shook off its drowsiness. Some yawned. The final hymn was announced. By some error – Caleb never knew whose – the opening hymn was repeated, and once again the rallying cry went forth.

'When all thy mercies, O my God…'

It was a fine ending. Everyone sang with as much gusto as ever, and rather more, for they all rejoiced that the service was over and fresh air was just outside.

They came out of church like bees out of a hive, buzzing and hovering around the door for a little while before disappearing. Only one worshipper seemed in a real hurry to get home. But nobody noticed him – unless we count the pedlar. That strange uncouth man stood looking about him, and then smiled secretly to himself as he saw Woodrow's head and shoulders above the churchyard wall. The apothecary was evidently having to struggle hard against the encumbering snow.

Ten: A filthy worsted-stocking knave

Mr Josiah Woodrow burst into his shop with a flurry of snow-flakes and dashed his hat on to the counter.

'Sam!' he yelled. 'Sam, you young felon! Come here!'

The lad appeared, hardly changed since his earlier entrance. He grinned vacantly.

'How's this?' demanded Woodrow angrily.

'Eh?' Sam stared at him. 'How's what?'

'What were you doing last night?'

'Eh?' asked Sam. 'Doin'?'

'What 'appened last night?'

'Happened? I told thee, didn't I?'

The apothecary took a step across the shop and seized him by the throat, his thumbs pressing into the boy's windpipe.

'Then tell me again. Just what happened?'

'Take them 'ands off me!' yelled the lad, getting a grip on the man's wrists and twisting them violently away. 'I'll be the death o' thee, Mr Woodrow! I'm warning thee. I'll be the death o' thee!'

But he backed away towards the inner door and watched the apothecary warily, as if he expected another attack.

'Tell me!' thundered Woodrow. 'What happened down in the churchyard last night?'

' 'Appened?' queried Sam again.

'Yes, you numbskull! What happened?'

'Just what I said.'

'You left him lying there?' queried Woodrow, eyeing the boy closely.

'Aye. He were lying flat in t' grass.'

'You're sure?'

'I seed 'im.'

'What about the man who came?'

'Aye. Well, I told thee. I heard a shout, and it were from a man, up by t' church, a long way off. So I hit hard, and ran away through t' hedge into t' field.'

'Did this man see you?'

'Not close to. Come to that, I never seed 'im proper, neither.'

'And young Tankard?'

'I left 'im theer. On t' ground.'

'Was he stunned?'

'Stunned or dead. Dead, I reckon. I hit 'im like this – thump! And again – thump! – like that. Full swing o' the stick – reet hard! And down he went.'

'And what about the stick?'

'I threw it down, just as tha said, reet near him.'

Woodrow kept looking at the boy and thinking.

'You wouldn't play tricks on me, Sam?'

'Tricks? I en't playing no tricks. It's just as I said – I hit 'im.'

Woodrow kept drilling him with his eyes.

'When did you take those pills to old Tankard?'

'Five minutes after I came back from t' churchyard.'

'You didn't stop anywhere?'

'No. I went straight to the house. Cross me 'eart.'

'Well, it's very odd, Sam, because nobody found a thing in the churchyard. No lad, not even Dickinson's stick.'

'I left 'im lying there,' Sam declared, stubbornly. 'An' that stick, too.'

'Well, someone must have moved them both. For Dickinson's walking about, free as the air.'

A slow grin spread over Sam's face.

'Eh!' he said, poking a finger towards the apothecary. ''E's found thee out! 'E knows who's done it. An' tha thought tha were clever, Mr Woodrow. He, he!'

'Take that smile off your face,' threatened the man. 'He knows nothing.'

'Tankard – he's clever,' laughed Sam. 'He'll 'ave thee strung up. He'll 'ave thee dancin' on a rope. Ha ha!'

'You young devil!' snapped Woodrow. 'Get out! Any tricks out of you and I'll slit your throat.'

*

Meanwhile, the vicar, wearied after his exertions in the pulpit, was leaning back in his tall chair by the fireside. Gradually he became aware of a babble of voices from the kitchen, angry women's voices.

'Get out of 'ere! Take that foot off the step! Go on! Get away with thee! We don't want beggars here! Go on!'

'But, my dear ladies…' protested a voice.

The vicar opened his eyes.

'Don't "dear ladies" us! We en't dear ladies. Get out o' t' kitchen. I'll clout thee with this broom if tha don't! And I've clouted bigger ones than thee! I'll clout thee hard, I'm warning thee.'

'Dear, dear ladies!' protested the voice, which was rich and musical.

Entering the kitchen, the vicar beheld three of his ancient helpers thrusting and chopping with broom handles and shovels at some would-be intruder.

'Stop! Stop!' he entreated. But the defenders were deaf to calls for peace.

'Widow Heddlestone!' he tried again, taking hold of a broomstick as it was raised to strike. 'Widow Heddlestone! What are you about?'

'Let go!' she cried, struggling to free her weapon. Then, turning and discovering who it was who had intervened, she immediately made an apologetic bob. 'Oh, sir! I never knew it were thee, sir.'

She meekly allowed herself to be disarmed, at which her fellow combatants also fell back into the kitchen and stood there sheepishly, pushing the fallen wisps of hair out of their eyes.

'What is going on?' demanded the vicar.

'It's 'im – yon!' panted Widow Heddlestone, pointing at the pedlar, who stood out in the yard, his arms still half-raised in an attitude of defence.

'Tried to come in,' panted one of the others.

'Reet impert'nent!' panted the third, endeavouring to hide an incriminating shovel behind her skirts.

The vicar looked at the ragged figure outside and recalled having seen him earlier in the congregation.

'What do you mean by alarming my servants?' he demanded sternly. 'I'll have you know I'll suffer none of my flock to be insulted, be they young or old, rich or poor. So, my man, what is your business?'

'I merely begged a few words with the incumbent,' said the pedlar.

'I am the incumbent,' the vicar informed him. 'I must also warn you that I am a Justice of the Peace.'

'May I begin, sir,' said the pedlar, 'by saying how sorry I am to have upset your household.'

As he spoke, the others stared at him. For his cultured accents were completely out of keeping with his appearance. 'But these good women,' he continued, 'no doubt mistaking me for an idle fellow – for which I don't blame them – hardly gave me the chance to explain myself.'

The short-sighted vicar peered at him, puzzled to know what sort of a person could be addressing him so. Minister of religion and Justice of the Peace fought for supremacy in his breast. Eventually the minister won. He bade the stranger scrape his boots and step inside.

'Now then,' said Mr Openshaw, shutting the door. 'What business brings you here?'

The pedlar looked about him and noted the litter of books, the musical instruments and the massive old Bible on the table.

'I was in your church this morning,' he began. Then his gaze fell upon a tall bassoon leaning against the side of the chair. 'I was impressed by the service.'

The vicar peered at him again, frowning. 'You are a strange man to be a pedlar,' he observed.

'Some would say I'm a strange man, whether a pedlar or not,' replied the stranger with a twinkle in his blue eyes.

'You don't speak like a pedlar,' said the vicar, looking askance at the battered old tricorn hat and the traces of stabling on the man's varied attire.

'Ah, Y'Reverance,' smiled the pedlar, and he was now a pedlar indeed. 'I'm just a poor man.' He swung his pack from his shoulder. 'Won't you just look at my wares for a minute, sir?' His long fingers pulled open the straps which held the flap. 'Here's a bit o' fine Irish linen. Just feel the quality o' that, sir! Feel it for yourself. Now, I don't need to tell a gentleman like you, sir, that it's linen fit for the gentry, the very finest money can buy – when money can buy it. And you're in luck, sir, to be told that money can indeed buy it today, and that I'm ready to sell it at only half the price I paid for it.'

The vicar, having no desire to make any purchases either that day or any other, tried to hand the material back to him, but the pedlar made sure his customer continued holding it and feeling it between his fingers as he was bidden; nor was the vicar given a chance to voice his refusal. As soon as he opened his mouth, the pedlar continued, 'Now, you were about to ask me how I can afford to sell cheaper than I buy. The truth is, of course, that I lose on the deal. I actually go around losing money.'

Again the vicar tried to speak but was waved into silence.

'Times are bad; I am forced into it,' lamented the pedlar, pulling a long face. 'But that's my affair. Here am I offering you the finest Irish linen at half the price. It's my misfortune, but it's your good fortune.'

He smiled reassuringly, then continued with his patter.

'I'll tell you a secret, Y'Reverance. I shouldn't really, because this is confidential. But,' he began, lowering his voice and glancing over his shoulder, 'the Prince of Wales himself has sent a special messenger to me, begging for enough of this linen to make ten shirts. He implored me; but I'll have to disappoint him. My credit's not good and I can't afford to outlay. That's the worst of being a poor man. The poor must remain poor for lack of a shilling.'

'Dear me,' said the vicar, at last finding a use for his tongue. 'This is a terrible situation. You actually have a request from His Royal Highness? My poor fellow! I must see what I can do!'

At which the pedlar laughed aloud and restrained his host from searching immediately for some ready money.

'No, no, sir,' he said in a changed voice. Then, picking up the bassoon which had so engrossed his attention, he put his lips to the double reed and fingered a little tune.

The poor vicar was utterly bewildered. He seemed to be dealing with two people in one body, and being unused to such things, he could only blink and gape and scratch his head.

'Oh! But my hands are cold!' exclaimed the stranger, replacing the bassoon and rubbing his mittened hands vigorously. As he did so, he glanced at the grate, where the few coals were rapidly burning out.

'You are indeed an extraordinary man,' declared the vicar.

'So I must confess,' said the stranger numbly. 'And I come to you under an assumed guise. I am no more a pedlar than you are yourself. And as for my cheapjack's patter, I have never sold a pin nor a button in my life.'

The vicar was more amazed than ever.

'But in putting aside this cloak and dissembling,' went on his visitor, 'I throw myself entirely upon your indulgence and discretion. It was foolish of me perhaps, to have allowed even those ancient beldames in your kitchen – and, odds life! What a trio they would be in *Macbeth*! – to have heard me speaking in my own voice. But I was under the stress of physical assault, and I fancy they were too engrossed to notice. Believe me, however, I have an honest reason for my deceit.'

'If you are not a pedlar, then,' asked the vicar, 'who are you?'

The stranger shrugged his shoulders.

'My name matters little,' he said. 'In my time I have played many parts and assumed many names. At present I am playing the part of Abel Bungeham, a worthy man, a loquacious man, rather down at heel, but an honest fellow withal.'

'Playing a part, Mr Bungeham? Am I to understand—?'

'No, sir,' smiled his visitor, 'you are not to understand. You are merely to accept the fact.'

'You speak in riddles,' sighed the vicar, 'and I still don't know what you want.'

'Ah!' said Bungeham. 'I come to you because you are a man I feel I can trust. You believe in justice and you are interested in the hidden things of darkness.'

'Indeed!' gasped Mr Openshaw, looking up sharply. 'Do you know something about last night?'

'Nothing save what is rumoured, and what my intelligence can piece together. But you, sir,' he pointed directly at the vicar, 'know considerably more.'

Mr Openshaw was caught off guard. 'You amaze me!' he stammered. 'I don't know what to say.'

'Trust me,' urged Bungeham. 'If there has been violence, there might yet be more. By telling me all you can, you might help me prevent it, although I cannot vouchsafe to do so. But let me explain: I am here on behalf of certain gentlemen in London. Things have happened in one or two places which have greatly perturbed them. They fear for the safety of the realm.'

'You are a government spy?' suggested the vicar in tones of horror.

'On the contrary,' declared the pedlar. 'These gentlemen of whom I speak are most anxious to denounce the employment of spies. And it is because we suspect you have a most treacherous spy in your midst that I am here.'

'A spy? Here?'

Mr Bungeham nodded. 'But with your help, Reverend, sir, we shall unmask him. Now, tell me what you know.'

The vicar related how Caleb had been attacked and explained why he had suppressed the story.

'Excellent! You did well, sir!' Bungeham exclaimed. 'Observe now this all corroborates my suspicions. Unless you had acted as you have done, our spy would still have held the whip hand. But now, he is in a very unhappy position. He has lost the initiative. He believes he left young Jeremy badly injured or dead, but doesn't know what has become of him.'

'Nor do we,' confessed the vicar sadly. 'The poor lad has yet to be found.'

'Not at all,' Bungeham reassured him. 'We know exactly where he is.'

'We do?' The vicar's face lit up.

'Well, I do!' corrected Mr Bungeham. 'He's at the first posting house on the Manchester road, and probably having an excellent lunch at this very moment.'

'At a posting house?'

'Don't imagine I contrived to send him there,' explained Bungeham. 'He went of his own accord.'

'This is excellent news! What a relief! We must tell his uncle at once.'

'Now just a minute,' cautioned the other. 'Let us go carefully. There may be more important things just now than Mr Tankard's peace of mind.'

'Come, come, sir,' remonstrated the vicar. 'We can't withhold news like this.'

'I think we can. And we must.'

'It would be very cruel.'

'No, sir. From what you have told me about Mr Tankard, I think we must keep silent. He has dealings with our spy, remember, or he wouldn't have come searching the graveyard. We must regard him as being in the enemy's camp.'

Reluctantly, the vicar agreed.

'Now,' said Bungeham. 'Let us consider this man Dickinson.'

Except that he was a friend of Caleb, the vicar knew little of him. 'Shall I call the lad in?' he asked.

'I think not. No, sir, I don't doubt your son's discretion, but the fewer who share a secret the better.'

The pedlar pondered what he had learned for a moment or two, then pushed back his chair and rose to his feet.

'I think I've detained you long enough,' he apologised. 'I'll go now. If you wish to find me, send word to the Packhorse. And remember, Y'Reverance,' he said, assuming once again the whine of the pedlar, 'I'm only a poor man. I'm not a man o' learning like you are, sir. I'm just a poor man, but an honest one.'

He backed out of the doorway and continued speaking in a loud voice so that all in the house could hear. 'Thank you, Y'Reverance. You're a gentleman, sir. God bless you!'

Eleven: Tardy-gaited knight

The day ended, but the two old watchmen who prowled the streets of Penkley were too feeble to afford security, and on this night, too cold to have thoughts beyond their own comfort. If someone was filling sacks at Tankard's coal heap, or bringing in a slain sheep from a nearby fold, or ripping out the woodwork from an empty house in the High Street, what did they care? And they were not at all anxious to meddle with a man who, by committing such offences, was liable to be hanged.

However, had they kept their eyes open, they might have seen first one, then two, and finally upwards of twenty men slinking down the lanes towards the waggoner's yard. They might have seen them enter by a wicket gate to the rear and climb a steep ladder up to a sort of window about fifteen feet above the ground in the gable of a large wooden shed.

Caleb Openshaw was among those who kept this mysterious tryst. Climbing the ladder, he stepped into the loft. The blackness within was impenetrable. As he groped inside, a hand seized his wrist and he felt something pressing against the bosom of his coat. He knew it was a knife.

'Adam delved,' he managed to gasp.

'Name?' asked a voice.

'Caleb.'

'Over to the right. Behind those sacks.'

He could see no sacks, but moved cautiously in the direction indicated, groping along the rough woodwork, afraid of crashing his injured head against a beam.

'Now, over to the left,' said another voice, 'and sit down.'

He stumbled over a man's foot. The man swore angrily, so Caleb sat down where he was and waited for his eyes to grow accustomed to the darkness. Gradually he discerned a circle of figures, some astride sacks, others lying on the floor, one squatting on a small box. Nobody spoke.

Then he heard the doorkeeper demanding the name of the next arrival, who soon came groping his way to their midst. Another half-dozen joined them. Then the doorkeeper pulled up the ladder outside and closed the door.

'All secure?' asked Dickinson, for it was he who sat upon the box.

The doorkeeper grunted assent.

'Good,' said Dickinson. 'I think we can light the lamps now!'

Set in the centre of the circle, the lamps threw great shadows on the walls. It was an uncanny scene – a small circle of lighted faces with blackness beyond.

Caleb glanced about him. What lined faces some of these had! The light made the creases so black and deep.

'Are we all here?' Dickinson asked.

'Nay. Wilfred Trimble can't come. His old mother's on her deathbed.'

'So I heard,' nodded Dickinson, with a hint of sympathy. 'But to begin… I declare this meeting of the Penkley Association of Free Men of England duly open.'

'Aye,' interrupted a little bald-headed man. 'But before we go further, Mr Dickinson—'

'Well, Simpkins?'

'I don't hold with yon lad being here.' He indicated Caleb.

'The lad's a sworn member just as you are, Simpkins.'

'Maybe. But I still don't hold with it.'

'Nay. Nor me, neither,' put in Jess Harthill, a big fellow with a woollen cap pulled over his ears. 'This is for workin' men, not lads.'

'Jess is reet,' interrupted another. 'We formed this Association for men from t' mill. We're all men from t' mill, bar yon lad. Now, if thar ask me—'

'Nay. That en't so,' declared Dickinson. 'This is an Association for Free Men. It's nowt to do wi' t' mill. Leastways, men who an't workin' in t' mill can join as much as t'others. There's our friend, Josiah Woodrow, for instance.'

'Aye, but he's a workin' man, like us,' argued Jess Harthill. 'Besides, we know Josiah and he's been a reet friend to us all. But yon lad – nay! – he's gentlefolk, and we don't want no gentlefolk.'

'May I say a word, hinny?' interposed Woodrow politely.

'Aye, let's hear Josiah. Speak up, man.'

'I'm very flattered by what you say about me, Jess,' smiled Woodrow, his teeth gleaming in the light. 'But I feel you are a little hard on our young comrade. Didn't John Dickinson himself make him a member?'

'Aye, maybe so,' agreed Jess, 'and I don't mean the lad no harm. But I an't forgotten last Friday neet.'

'And what has last Friday to do wi't' lad?' asked Dickinson.

'Don't forget it were this lad's father as sent Joss Barker for trial. An' more than that,' went on Harthill, 'it were this lad's schoolfellow as let 'is tongue wag.'

'That's not true!' declared Caleb angrily.

'Ee, now,' accused Harthill, 'if it en't as plain as the nose on tha face, what is?'

'Jeremy never said a word about Joss,' retorted Caleb.

'Tha'll never make me believe that,' sneered Harthill.

'We'll leave our discussing that until the lad in question can answer for hissen,' said Dickinson. 'I have my own views on this matter, and I feel as strong as tha does, Jess Harthill, but it don't reflect on Caleb here.'

'Thank you, Mr Dickinson,' said Caleb, 'but I must make it quite plain about Jeremy. He never said a thing, not a word. I know he didn't.'

'Ah! Tha knows!' sneered Harthill, losing his temper. 'Tha knows too much, tha does. Young Tankard knew too much also. If he hadn't known so much, Joss Barker 'ud be a free man today.'

'Hear, hear, Jess!' chipped in the bald man. 'We don't need gentlefolk. Tha can't trust them.'

'Now, before we lose our tempers,' interrupted Woodrow, quietly, 'perhaps we could give the boy a chance to speak. He states he knows his friend is innocent. Don't you think we ought to listen to him, and give him the chance to prove it?'

'Reet!' said Harthill. 'Come on, lad. Prove it.'

'I can prove it because I know what sort of person Jeremy is,' said Caleb. 'He isn't the sort who tells tales. He wouldn't do anything like that. It just isn't Jeremy.'

His words were drowned in the mocking laughter of the men.

'Hear him!' declared Harthill. 'His schoolmate wouldn't carry tales because his schoolmate doesn't do things like that. A fine sort of proof!' The bald man spat on the dusty floor.

'Tankards!' he said 'Tankards! Like uncle, like nephew!'

'You haven't seen your friend, then?' asked Woodrow, in a judicial manner.

'Not since yesterday morning,' Caleb explained. 'He left in the middle of lessons, and no one's seen him since.'

'And I'm accused of killing him,' said Dickinson bitterly.

'Pity nobody did kill him,' said Harthill.

'Come, come!' Woodrow rebuked him. 'We are an Association of Free Men, not of murderers.'

'Aye,' agreed Dickinson. 'We'll have none o' that talk. If it comes to fighting, we'll fight honest. And as for my friend here, young Openshaw, I'll vouch for him personally. I'm afraid I can't vouch for his schoolmate because I've never trusted the lad meself. But young Caleb is as true as steel. If it weren't for him, we wouldn't be gathered here tonight. I'd have no means of reaching you, save by going round from house to house, and we don't want that, do we? And we don't want to have to whisper messages in alehouses, and that sort of thing. But nobody'll ever suspect us if we keep on singing our messages in church. Yet to do that, we need young Caleb.'

'Our President's a good man,' said Woodrow, 'and I think we must accept his word. As he says, we have excellent arrangements. We all know what to do when the right hymns are sung.'

'Aye,' said Simpkins, 'but when will the right hymns be sung?'

'We've waited too long for them,' said a morose man who had not hitherto spoken. 'I've half a loaf of bread at home, and two ounces of cheese. What happens tomorrow when that's gone? Does the parish keep me? Or do I starve?'

'I've given thought to that,' said Dickinson, 'and I've been to see Tankard on your behalf.'

'Don't bother tellin' us,' interrupted Harthill. 'He wouldn't listen, of course. And I don't blame him. There was no sense in that scheme o' thine, as I told thee.'

'It were worth a try,' said Dickinson.

'It were damn nonsense,' said the bald man.

Dickinson bridled with sudden anger. 'No, it weren't! If us workin' men all over England were to stick together and get possession of all the fields and ironworks and cotton mills, we could work them for our own benefit. We have the skill and the muscle.'

'Aye, that's so,' agreed the bald man, 'but we'd have to seize 'em by main force. We'd never get 'em by asking nicely and seeking to rent them. Nay! Yon gentry folk and mill owners will never let the likes of us get hands on their property. Can you imagine they would? If they did, they'd stop being gentry folk, and they knows it.'

'That's it,' came in Harthill. 'They knows it. And if we're ever to get hands on their mills and things, we'll have to fight 'em. Make no mistake about it, we've got to fight 'em. So let's sing the right hymn this next week and get all our lads out. Do it on a Sunday when there's no coaches running and news travels slow. Burn old Tankard out. Storm the mill!'

'Harthill! You're a reet fool!' came a voice from the shadows on the other side.

'Call me a fool, do you, Matthew Oakes?'

'Aye, I do! The cavalry 'ud be in Penkley before tha'd marched a mile. The lot o' ye 'ud be hanged and nowt gained, save a lot o' new widows and orphans.'

'Tha's reet, Matthew,' said Will Hampson, next to Caleb. 'Bonyparte had to give in to t' redcoats. I don't think Jess Harthill 'ud do better.'

Woodrow gave a little laugh. 'You have a point there, Will, hinny,' he remarked. 'But when things are hard and there seems no way of mending them except by making the sort of proposition John Dickinson is suggesting, it might be better to risk the redcoats than starve to death. If I take Jess Harthill's meaning right, he wants a show of force merely to compel Tankard to listen to John. Is that it, Jess?'

'Well,' said Jess, 'I'm not so sure—'

'Certainly that would be the wisest course,' Woodrow went on. 'For after all, if you could obtain a lease on the mill, become your own masters, and your own men, you wouldn't have to listen to what a mill owner ordered. You wouldn't have to pay fines any more.'

'*Fines!*' exploded Harthill in anger. 'Sixpence for having a window ajar, if only by the thickness of a finger, and the air so foul one can hardly breathe! Sixpence for being a minute late! I tell thee, Matthew Oakes, the black slaves are better off than us.'

'That's true,' rejoined the bald man. 'Wherever there's mills, there's slaves. But it only wants the slaves in one town to raise the flag and throw off their shackles, and the rest'll follow. These mill owners know that better than us, and they're frightened, I tell thee. The lot of 'em are frightened. If we in Penkley took the law into our own hands, the whole country 'ud follow us. It just needs a spark to the powder.'

'I'm sure that's true,' said Harthill, 'and nowt'll get better if we do nowt. Things'll only get worse. Besides, what have we to lose?'

'Our lives,' Matthew Oakes was quick to tell him, 'and the lives of our families.'

'Lives!' sneered Harthill. 'What's life here? Starvation! Cold! At least, if Tankard's house burnt down, we could get our hands warm.'

'I don't think burning places would be very helpful,' said Dickinson. 'Nay, I'll have another try at reasoning with the man. I've told Tankard we're reasonable folks, and I want him to see we are.'

'Tha were reet,' said Matthew Oakes.

'But I warned him what might happen,' added Dickinson. 'So perhaps, if he's still obstinate at the end of the week after seeing how reasonable everyone's been, then we might give him a hint of trouble – a crowd at his house, perhaps, a few stones through his windows. But let's draw the line at that.'

'Stones through his windows!' exclaimed Harthill. 'What good would that do? It's fire he needs. It's terror. We want to set the place ablaze and burn the old miser in his bed.'

'No, no! Not bloodshed,' warned Woodrow. 'I will never advocate bloodshed. It wouldn't help our friend Joss Barker when he comes up for trial.'

'Nowt can help him,' retorted Harthill. 'They've got the noose round his neck already. But if he's hanged or transported, I won't rest until I've avenged him. I'll see old Tankard gets his deserts, that I will. And young Tankard, too, if he hasn't got them already.'

'Joss were a fool,' declared Simpkins. 'Joss opened his mouth too wide. Dead reet, of course. He knew things, did Joss. Fought against the French. But he fought on t' wrong side. Them Frogs knew what they was about, chopping all yon heads off – king, queen, and all them in the fancy breeches. We'd ha' done it now. Put old King Lud on the throne! That's what we need.'

'Happen it'll come to that,' said Dickinson. 'In good time. Man was born free, someone has said, but everywhere he's in chains. That's true in Penkley reet enough. And it's up to us to change it. No one else will.'

'It's better to be careful, Mr Dickinson,' warned Woodrow. 'All the power of the state is against us, don't forget. But if trouble comes, it might as well come in winter. Snow and frost make movement difficult. Look what it did to Boney in Russia.'

'Aye. Tha needs to remember that, John Dickinson,' said the bald man. 'We could act safely if the roads were blocked. It's worth a thought.'

'True!' agreed Dickinson. 'It's worth a thought. So, if the snow continues, and I fail to make a deal for the mill with Tankard, then a demonstration would best be arranged for next Sunday night. Do we agree? But you must wait for my signal, and only then get everyone out. But, remember – no bloodshed, and no fire. Then when I give the word, I want everyone back home again as quickly as possible. We want to frighten the man, no more.'

'Agreed,' said Oakes approvingly.

The rebel faction was not so enthusiastic.

'It'll come to open war in the end,' said the bald man.

'Let's bide our time, then,' urged Woodrow. 'I have every confidence in Mr Dickinson. He wants us to preserve our lives so that we may enjoy the fruits of victory.'

'Do we agree on what I propose, then?' asked Dickinson.

Although there were some mumblings to indicate that not everyone was convinced of the merit of his suggestion, no one voiced any objection.

'Good. Then await the signal. And welcome all who would valiant be!'

Twelve: Icicles by the wall

The snow lay like a shroud over Penkley, for the town was dead. For the next few days nothing came in, nothing went out, and every place of industry was closed.

The great communal grave which old Kinch laboured to hack out of the frozen earth was like an omen. All Monday he toiled at it, wielding pick and shovel, and pausing after every few strokes to rest. Wise in the ways of cruel winter, old Kinch did his work unbidden. The vicar watched him from the vicarage windows and made no comment. Others who saw him hurried away with a shudder and wondered how long it would be before larger pits were required.

Cold hit the town cruelly. Food was short and hunger added its pains. But there was little talk among the majority of Penkley people of rights and rebellion. Most of them had heard that Mr Dickinson would try again to reason with their employer, but confidence in Mr Dickinson was vanishing with the last few victuals.

Some of the younger men were neither docile nor inactive. Their families found their cottage fires well stocked with strange billets bearing the marks of carpentry – some with locks and hinges attached. No one asked questions should there be feathers in an outhouse or a woolly fleece beneath a mattress.

At the apothecary's shop, Sam had procured a butcher's cleaver. It chopped sticks for the fire admirably. It might even, as he observed to his master, 'Chop an 'ead open, if you like.'

Josiah Woodrow, that great advocate of good sense and moderation, looked critically at the oblong blade and nodded his agreement.

'Get a good swing on that, Sam, hinny, and you'd split a man in half.'

The idea appealed to his assistant. He chopped at an imaginary opponent, saying, 'Ee, that 'ud finish him.'

'And you, too,' said Woodrow.

'Nar!' objected Sam. 'I'd 'ave 'im afore 'e know it.'

'But if he were armed?' asked the apothecary. 'Suppose he had a knife.'

'Aye, and suppose he had?'

'While you were raising your weapon, he'd attack you in the front.'

Sam considered the matter. 'Aye, maybe he would,' he conceded. 'Happen I need a shield.'

'Or a knife in your left hand. That used to be the old way of fencing.'

Sam picked up a poker to see how a second weapon might be used. 'Aye, I'll get me a knife, too. Then I'm all ready.'

He practised a little shadow-fencing, parrying thrusts from daggers and delivering knockout blows with the cleaver. He had no doubt he would prove invincible.

'Pity I didn't use this cleaver on little Tankard,' he said.

'Pity you didn't,' returned Woodrow, irritably. 'Leastways, I'd know he was dead.'

'He's dead reet enough,' declared Sam. 'And somebody's hiding the body.'

'And I've a feeling,' added Woodrow grimly, 'it's that vicar.' He looked at Sam enquiringly. 'Can't you think who it was who shouted across to you?'

'As tha says, it might ha' been t'owld sexton,' said Sam. 'But I never stopped to find out.'

'Supposing it was the sexton,' pursued Woodrow, speaking more to himself than to Sam, 'what's the game? What are they trying to do?'

'I can tell thee that,' grinned Sam. 'They're trying to put a noose round tha neck. And I bet old Tankard knows all about it. I bet he knows who left yon babbie on his step, too. He'll hang thee yet, Mr Woodrow. He's just biding his time.'

'He's not,' smiled Woodrow. 'He brought me here. He paid me money to come. Without me he wouldn't know a thing. He relies on me.'

'So tha'll tell him about next Sunday, will thee?'

'Maybe. In good time, when it's too late for him to do much.

After all, we want to see him roast on his own griddle, don't we? When I told Lord Sidmouth there'd be trouble, I meant trouble.'

Sam thought this was all highly comical.

'Ee! Yon's a grand idea. We'll make Tankard dance, shall we? You and me?'

'He'll dance all right,' smiled Woodrow. Then the smile died from his lips, and he snatched up the cleaver which Sam had absent-mindedly set down on the counter. 'Now, boy!' he thundered. 'Who told you about yon babbie?'

Sam stared at the edge of the cleaver not two inches in front of his nose.

'I looked in t' box,' he said. 'Didst know they buries yon in t' churchyard?'

'You're a damned little spy!' breathed Woodrow between his teeth. 'Watch out you don't poke your nose out too far.'

Sam laughed. 'Meg Wooller's babbie, weren't it?' he asked. 'She that died a week agone. I knew her babbie wouldn't live long.'

'See you keep your mouth shut!' snapped the apothecary. 'If not, your head'll be the first to test *this*.' With a sudden blow, he struck the corner of the cleaver deep in the counter, and left the implement standing up at an acute angle.

'Nay!' Sam managed to say after he had recovered from the surprise. 'Tha won't do that! Who'd lead the lads if I weren't there? Who'd throw yon bottles o' thine?'

'Not a word about those,' warned the apothecary.

Sam was looking under the counter at four dark green bottles which stood at the end of the shelf.

'Hast prepared t' linstock yet?' he asked slyly.

'All in good time,' nodded his master. 'Everything'll be ready on the day. And you'll be there, leading the lads on, setting the whole place ablaze, and having a rare old time.'

Sam rubbed his hands together in gleeful anticipation.

'I'll have a time, Mr Woodrow!' he grinned. 'I'll have a reet time! The best time I've ever had. I'll be quit with them Tankards for what they've done to me, Mr Woodrow! I'll be quit with everyone. I'll be top dog this time. I'll be cock o' t' midden. I'll make 'em grovel!'

*

But if Sam was delighted with the prospects ahead, other folk in Penkley were not so happy. Mr Openshaw, for instance, was filled with foreboding. On the Tuesday morning he went across the town to the Gable House. After he had repeatedly knocked at the door, Tankard himself admitted him. The mill owner was haggard, unshaven, without his neckcloth, and with the knee buckles on his breeches unfastened.

'Well? What news?' he demanded hoarsely.

The vicar felt deeply sorry for him, and was sorely tempted to end his uncertainties by telling him the news about Jeremy. But the words of his strange visitor, the mysterious pedlar, made him guard his tongue.

'Nothing,' he replied, and lifted a silent prayer seeking forgiveness for the untruth.

The mill owner sighed. All the breath of his body seemed to escape.

'The lad's dead,' he muttered.

'Ah! Never give up hope,' the vicar was quick to tell him. 'You don't know he's dead.'

Tankard gave a mirthless laugh.

'Do you suppose he's wandering the hills?' he asked bitterly. 'Three days out in the open in this weather! Come, Vicar. Don't delude thyself. The lad's dead. Let's face it.'

Mr Openshaw made no reply, but looked down at the floor.

'Well? What hast tha come for?' asked the mill owner with surly impatience. 'Not to give spiritual consolation, I hope?'

'Yes, if you wished it. But if not, I wanted to discuss what we as magistrates might do for the poor people. They'll die if this snow continues.'

'Now, don't blame me for t' snow,' retorted the mill owner. 'If there's owt to be done in that line, it's tha province.'

The vicar smiled sadly before saying, 'Of course, these people are all in my care.'

'Well, I'm reet glad to hear that!' exploded Tankard. 'People are mostly telling me they're all in mine, as if they were my flock. "Get work started again," they say, and, "Rent mill to t' workers."

112

As if I or anyone else can alter prices and sell goods where there's no demand! But everyone seems to think I can. They think I ought to make work and pay wages out of empty coffers, though they never tell me how. So it's a relief to know that the people are in your care, Mr Vicar, and the load's on your shoulders and not on mine.'

The vicar ignored this outburst and said very simply, 'The people need food.'

'That's your care,' pointed out Tankard, shrugging his shoulders.

'When the Lord said, "Feed my lambs",' said the vicar, 'I'm sure he meant it in all senses.'

'No doubt,' said the mill owner, 'and it's upon you to go and do as you are told. But don't come here. 'Ten't my business, and even if it were, I've nowt to feed 'em with. There's nowt but a half-quarten loaf in my larder, and that's going mouldy. The old woman's off her head – and no wonder, the place is like it is.' He looked wildly around as is he had completely lost control of things.

'Are there no stocks of food in the town?' asked the vicar.

'Go and ask the corn chandler! I'm in the cotton trade myself.'

The hard-headed practical man and the dreamer seemed to have changed places. The vicar frowned with exasperation.

'Then if you haven't food, Mr Tankard, perhaps you've money.'

'Ah! So that's it?' The mill owner looked at him suspiciously. 'I knew you'd pass the job over to me. You say the care of the people is your responsibility. You are the one to feed tha lambs. But in the end, you want me to do it for you. I've to foot the bill.'

'Parish funds are almost exhausted.'

'You spend too much on communion wine.'

'You could make a loan to the parish, and I could buy grain for distribution.' The vicar looked imploringly at his fellow magistrate. 'Remember that in feeding the five thousand, our Lord had first to borrow the loaves and fishes.'

Tankard pouted his lips. He took a full minute to consider his reply.

'Very well,' he said. 'I'll make a loan. Tell the dealers I'll underwrite whatever purchases you make. But I'll hold the vestry and churchwardens responsible for full repayment.'

The vicar's face lit up. 'This is splendid, Mr Tankard, splendid! An answer to my prayers.'

'Don't be such a damn fool!' growled the mill owner. 'I'm making a *loan*, not a gift. Although I'm not demanding interest, I'll hope you'll stop a fever breaking out, which is in interest enough. This isn't charity, it's business.'

As he was speaking, another knock sounded on the door. The two men had moved no further than the passage, and the knock sounded directly behind them.

'Callers come one after the other,' remarked Tankard. 'My popularity is soaring.' He turned round and bellowed, 'Who's there?'

'John Dickinson.'

The blood rose to Tankard's face. 'Go away!' he yelled. 'Get away before I clap thee in irons.'

'I made you a proposal,' said Dickinson. 'Have you considered it?'

'Proposal? From a murderer? Get your foot off my step!'

'I came to tell you, Mr Tankard,' Dickinson went on, 'it would be well to consider what I proposed more carefully. There are hotheads in the town.'

'Ho, ho!' thundered Tankard, rubbing his hands with delight. 'More threats? Carry on, Mr Engineer. Threaten me again. Keep on – and you, Mr Openshaw, keep your ears well open!'

'I am not threatening, merely warning, Mr Tankard. There are lots of angry men in this town who are not half so reasonable as I am.'

'Ho, ho! Hear that? Warning me? Not threatening, mark you. Oh, dear me, no.'

'John Dickinson!' Mr Openshaw called.

'Who's speaking?'

'The vicar. I've been consulting with Mr Tankard over the situation.'

'Then urge him to see sense, Your Reverence. Ask him to try my scheme. I'm not saying it'll be successful, but it's worth a try.'

'It's worth nowt!' declared the mill owner with contempt.

'John Dickinson,' the vicar went on, 'listen to me. Mr Tankard is supplying money to buy food. So tell this to your friends. And I'll see what else can be done.'

'Well, that's one thing,' said Dickinson, 'but what about my proposal?'

'You've had the answer!' yelled Tankard. Then, taking a deep breath, thundered out such a tremendous 'No!' that old Martha darted out into the passage in a blind panic, stopped and stood trembling for a moment with her eyes staring, before darting back again into the kitchen.

When the vicar called out Dickinson's name in an endeavour to heal some of the damage, there was no response. The snow had deadened his departing footfalls.

For a man who was by nature retiring and impractical, Mr Openshaw excelled himself that day. He called on everyone he guessed might have provisions. And having done business with them – not always easily, for they were hard bargainers, these Penkley folk – he enlisted a little band of helpers – Caleb and old Kinch to begin with, then Dickinson, then the ostler and Abel Bungeham from the inn, where he also procured the grudging use of two horses – and with these set out on his errands of mercy.

These were only interrupted for a brief spell when the vicar and Kinch went to perform the necessary rites over two of the flock who had departed this life in the freezing hours of the preceding morning. Otherwise, they were continuously engaged in the dwellings of the millhands. This was no pleasant task, for besides the filth and stench of ordure running in discoloured channels through the snow, there was the open hostility of many of the parishioners. A fair majority of his flock, male and female alike, were more wolves than sheep. Even the children were not averse to spitting at their shepherd and calling him obscene names.

There was little gratitude even when the laden horses came slipping up with their loads, and Dickinson began to distribute oatmeal and dried beans to the scramble. No one thanked the vicar. No one even thanked Dickinson. If any emotion was displayed, it was anger that someone had gained a larger share or been dealt with out of turn.

When the sacks were empty and the horses were turned about, there was violent animosity from those who for the time being had been left empty-handed. They cursed their benefactors with every vile word their tongues could muster. Stones were thrown, and one, hitting a horse on the flank, caused it to shy and whinny. Bungeham had to restrain the ostler from turning back and using his fists on the culprit.

Bungeham worked hard that day, too, and won the grudging respect of Dickinson, who normally had little time for tinkers and pedlars and suchlike wastrels. But he found Bungeham a pleasant and willing fellow, and they exchanged pleasantries as they humped sacks out of granaries and led horses up and down narrow lanes.

The work did not end that day, nor the next. But as more snow came down and yet more, the difficulties mounted. To the vicar it seemed they could hardly get worse, and yet they did. The corn merchants lifted their prices so high he could no longer afford to buy, once Tankard, having seen the bills, refused to support the grain distribution any further. The two magistrates had an acrimonious meeting at the Gable House and the vicar came away angry and dispirited.

The bitter weather was already taking a sad toll of the weak and aged of the town. The communal grave was already filling up. In the burial service, the expression 'our dear brothers and sisters here departed' was now the rule rather than the exception. Caleb, looking out of the window at the bent white head of his father, worried to see how old and frail he was.

The lad helped to the best of his abilities in whatever work was being done, and thus had several opportunities to talk with Dickinson.

'It can't go on like this,' said the engineer. 'There's food aplenty in the town, but the merchants are as bad as the mill owner.'

'Sunday?' asked Caleb.

'Sunday can't come soon enough.'

'I'll arrange it.'

'But I sincerely hope there'll be no bloodshed,' said Dickinson, and Caleb could detect behind the words the unspoken fear that bloodshed might be unavoidable.

*

Friday came, and into the inn yard strolled Sam, awkward in unaccustomed boots, a massive coat hiding his rags, and a monstrous fur cap on his head.

'What's here?' asked Bungeham, spying him from the parlour window. 'A Cossack?'

The Cossack came inside and loudly demanded a pot of ale.

'You're a fine fellow,' said Bungeham. 'I ain't seen tha likes o'you before.'

Sam looked at him with a superior air. Either the fur cap or the big coat had endowed him with a new dignity, so he despised mere pedlars.

When Bassenthwaite appeared, the lad produced a folded note.

'I want a horse,' he demanded.

The landlord looked at him enquiringly.

'Urgent business for Mr Woodrow,' said Sam importantly. 'He wants me to go to the next village.'

The landlord read the note carefully.

'I don't like trusting a horse to t' like o' thee,' he admitted.

The Cossack spun two golden coins on the counter.

'Mr Woodrow will pay for any damage. But 'tis urgent. Hast read t' letter?'

'Aye,' said Bassenthwaite glumly. 'But I don't like it. Roads is nigh impassable.'

'I'll get through,' Sam assured him. 'But Mr Woodrow needs – what did he say? – medicaments, urgent. That's the word – medicaments.' He cast another haughty look at the pedlar.

'I'll see what Joe thinks on it,' grumbled the landlord, and went out to the stables.

'You're a clever lad,' said the pedlar, once Bassenthwaite had gone.

Sam drained his mug and set it down with a flourish.

'Cleverer than thee, no doubt.'

'Aye?' asked Bungeham. 'How's that?'

'I can reet.'

'Can you, indeed? That's more than I can.'

'Aye, I can reet,' boasted the Cossack, pushing out his chest. Then he caught sight of Bessie.

'Here, lass! Fetch me pen and ink.'

'Eh?' Bessie blinked.

'Pen and ink, I said!'

She gave him an arch look, but at a nod from Bungeham went and brought them.

'Watch this,' said Sam, turning Woodrow's note on its face and dipping the quill in the inkhorn.

Bungeham watched, curious.

The lad put out his tongue as he scratched away, and the letters he formed were crude. His ungainly hands made the pen spit out ink at every turn. He was very slow, tackling the letters from the wrong end, as if they were drawings, and when he finally tossed down the pen with an air of triumph he had only written a few words.

'Aye!' Bungeham's tone revealed his admiration. 'You told the truth. You write fine, lad.'

Sam smiled with self-satisfaction.

The pedlar held the paper up and stared at it with an uncomprehending look, as a man might stare at a page of Hindustani. But he read it just the same.

'LET THE DED BURY THIR DED.'

'What does it say?' he asked.

Sam looked at him with scorn. 'What! Canst not read neither?' he asked. Then snatching the paper from the pedlar's hand, he tossed it into the fire.

The landlord came back, fidgety with misgivings, but prepared to hire out the horse as requested. Shortly afterwards, the Cossack was seen riding out of the yard on a short-legged pony, his ill-fitting boots sticking out in the stirrups on either side.

There was little to be done that day. The vicar went from dealer to dealer. Vestrymen though many of them were, they were unwilling to meet his terms. Now that the hour of need had struck, the parish organisation seemed to have shrunk to one man.

After a round of fruitless calls, the vicar went sadly home, but shortly afterwards was seen struggling down again through the snow. Over his shoulders was a sack, but not a very well-filled sack, and passers-by could hear its contents clinking as he walked.

On one of the street corners was a miserable pawnbroker's shop. The vicar went inside. One or two wretches were trying to gain a copper or two on trinkets which the pawnbroker could see at a glance were worthless, and he was being roundly abused for his parsimony. When they turned and saw who had entered, the flow of bad language ceased abruptly.

'Why, Mr Openshaw, sir! What can I do for thee?'

The vicar motioned him to the screen at the end of the counter.

'If I pledge these,' he asked as he tipped out the contents of the sack, 'what will you give me?'

The pawnbroker's eyes opened wide.

'Not these!' he gasped. 'Not these, Mr Openshaw!'

'They'll be redeemed,' the vicar assured him, and the word obviously echoed in his mind, for he stared in front of him as he repeated it. 'Redeemed!'

'But these are your personal treasures! Your bassoon! Your flute! Your clarinet!'

'I have more than this,' said the vicar, and from his pocket produced two gold rings.

'You can't, sir!'

'And these,' said the vicar in a hushed voice, feeling in the other pocket.

'No!' gasped the pawnbroker. 'Why! Aren't they—?'

'Yes. The communion plate.'

'But surely! Isn't it sacrilege? I mean—'

'Possibly it is,' said the vicar, 'but we won't go into the niceties. What will you give me?'

'I don't know what.' The pawnbroker scratched his head and stared at the miscellaneous objects on the counter.

'The money is most important,' said the vicar.

'I can't give much,' said the man in an agony of indecision. 'I haven't much to give.'

'Give what you can. And blessings be upon you.'

With five guineas in his hand, the vicar went out to see how best they could be spent.

Meanwhile Bassenthwaite and the ostler were anxiously awaiting the return of Sam, and the pony. When he eventually rode back into the yard, they almost knocked him out of the saddle in their haste to see if the animal was harmed.

'Did you get your medicaments?' asked the pedlar.

The Cossack's face was so frozen that he could do no more than nod, yet the pedlar noticed he was unburdened by any parcel or bag. Probably the medicaments were small enough to go into a pocket and not make a bulge.

'Any coach coming through yet?' Bungeham asked.

'There's nowt on t' roads,' replied the lad, pulling off his stiff gloves. 'I seed a big wagon abandoned by t' lower bridge, but nowt else.'

He rubbed his hands together vigorously, his face screwed up with the pain from his frozen joints.

'Ee! It's bad out yon! Great drifts – up to t' nag's belly!'

Bungeham sighed. Time was getting short.

*

Saturday came. The sky was blue and the air clear. Early in the morning, the pedlar trudged along to the vicarage. He was accepted now as a regular helper and the old women admitted him without question.

The vicar was in his private room, where a newly lit fire was sending up coils of thick smoke from the grate. As Bungeham entered, Mr Openshaw placed the heavy Bible on his threadbare knees and pulled his spectacles nearer the end of his nose. His eyes were bloodshot, his cheeks hollow. Bungeham was surprised to see how ill he looked.

'Aren't you well, sir?'

'A little tired,' smiled the parson. 'I'm a sedentary man. These last few days have fatigued me.'

'You need a rest. Parish relief is not your job. Let us handle it – Dickinson, the ostler, and me.'

'Pooh-pooh! Don't worry about me,' said the vicar. 'I enjoy myself. It's good to feel useful.'

Bungeham was not convinced. 'Well, just as you please,' he conceded. 'But I'd urge a little caution. This is severe weather, and overexertion isn't wise.'

'All the exertion is by you fellows, not by me. You've all answered the call splendidly. I'm very grateful.' He closed the Bible and replaced it on the table. 'Now! What have you come to see me about so early? You have breakfasted?'

'Very comfortably,' Bungeham assured him, 'sitting by the fire in the Packhorse.'

'Excellent.'

'I have called,' continued Bungeham, 'because I'm getting very anxious.'

'Anxious? Has something new come to light?'

'No. That's the point. I think something should have happened.'

'What did you expect?'

'Well, for one thing I had hoped young Blatchford would be here. I wrote to him a week ago. But the road must be blocked, and he's held up.'

'Very probably. No coaches have arrived all week.'

'And it's very frustrating. I had planned to use him to our advantage. I hope that doesn't sound too sinister. But now I can't see it being done.'

'I hope you weren't intending to endanger him.'

Bungeham smiled.

'I would never do that. No. I was preparing a simple ruse to uncover our spy. Of course, I know who the spy is. And Tankard knows – and His Majesty's Government knows, because he's on their payroll, sad to say. But the man needs exposing. I have to reveal him, not only as an informer, but as a liar, a mischief maker, a bearer of false witness. This may be no easy matter.'

'Couldn't I denounce him from my pulpit?'

'You probably would if I disclosed his name, but it would hardly achieve what I intend.'

'For the life of me, Bungeham,' said the vicar, 'I can't understand this business. Why should a man choose to dishonour himself by accepting so despicable a trade?'

'Despicable is right, sir.'

'But why should he follow it?' The vicar's frown revealed his puzzlement. 'I can understand many forms of criminal behaviour – theft, for instance.'

'Theft is a natural instinct, I would say.'

'Yes,' agreed the vicar thoughtfully, 'and in the last few days I have come to view it in a new light. I almost believe that on occasion there are people with a better right to property than the legal holder. Does that shock you, coming from a parson and a magistrate? But perhaps we don't make our Christianity shocking enough. And after all, did not Solomon say, "He that withholdeth corn, the people shall curse"?'

'And deservedly,' said Bungeham.

'But a spy!' exploded the vicar. 'A man seeking to pervert justice! A man living by bearing tales, by inventing stories, by cold-bloodedly plotting the discomfiture of his innocent fellows! What sort of a man is this? Why should a man choose to do things like this?'

'You expect me to give an answer?' asked Bungeham. 'You believe because I'm a child of this world, I must be wiser than the children of light?'

'Ah,' nodded the vicar. 'That's a perplexing text. We must discuss it some time.'

'In my opinion,' explained Bungeham, 'there are two motives at work. The first is greed for money. When a man is handsomely paid for the conviction of a felon, won't he seek felons out? And won't he – if he can't find any – set about making one or two? Then there is greed for power. When he realises he has the power of life and death in his hands, he uses it for sport.'

'This is monstrous!'

'Absolutely.'

'But,' the vicar said, blinking, 'are we governed by such knaves and fools that such things are allowed? Surely there are some honourable men in charge of our affairs? William Pitt was an upright man, was he not? Did he permit such things?'

'I cannot speak for William Pitt, nor for anyone else,' said Bungeham solemnly. 'I suppose every government must at times stoop to unsavoury methods. It is easy for us to condemn when we haven't the responsibility.'

'But you say the Government deliberately encourages spying?'

'They have no other means of gaining information. Spies are their protection – so they suppose. For there's always the possibility that someone may be plotting to assassinate the Cabinet, just as someone shot poor Percieval dead a few years ago.'

'Is the world as dreadful as that?' asked the parson.

Bungeham looked at him and marvelled. The innocence of the man! Where had he been throughout these last twenty-five terrible years when kings had lost their heads, countries been ravaged, and the fields and valleys of Europe choked with slaughtered men?

'These are terrible times!' sighed the vicar, shaking his head.

'And I seem thwarted in all my endeavours,' grumbled Bungeham. 'I told you our spy was off balance. I believed he would have toppled over by now, but he hasn't. I think he still needs a little push.'

'What sort of a push?'

'I haven't quite worked it out. But an idea came to me as I was talking to that lad who works for the apothecary. I think his name is Sam.'

'Yes. I know him. An uncouth, ungrateful fellow – but unfortunate. He was orphaned a year or two ago.'

'He's just been to the next village by pony,' said Bungeham. 'And it occurred to me – if he could get that far, why shouldn't we? And why shouldn't we purchase some supplies from the farms along the valley?'

'Excellent!' exclaimed the vicar. 'Excellent!' Then his face fell. 'But I've no more money!'

'I'll lend you some,' offered the pedlar, producing a little purse and shaking it to make the coins jingle.

The vicar's eyes lit up.

'And by the way,' said Bungeham, 'while I think of it. Have you ever seen a little text like this?'

He looked around for a sheet of paper, and when he found one, wrote on it the words, 'LET THE DED BURY THIR DED.'

The vicar stared at the words in amazement.

'Why, yes! I certainly have!'

'Ah!' said Bungeham. 'I felt sure it was significant. Perhaps you will tell me about it?'

He listened attentively as the vicar related what he knew about the box delivered to the Gable House and the child whose remains he had committed to the ground.

'Nothing is sacred to some folk,' commented Bungeham.

'A terrible message,' said the vicar. 'I suppose you know its author.'

'And his amanuensis. I fancy this same author has sent other messages, which even now might be triggering off some fresh mischief. I wonder if his amanuensis is fully aware of their contents.'

'There you go,' protested the vicar. 'Riddles again!'

'I am a veritable sphinx,' laughed Bungeham.

Thirteen: This is the man; do thy office

Joe, the ostler, knew all there was to know about horses and harness, but beyond this narrow range of knowledge, he was as ignorant as a caveman, and also stupid. Outside the stables he had no confidence in himself at all. He believed implicitly anything told him. Whatever people asked him to do, he did it. The man who was wise and shrewd when there was a horse beneath his hand was an utter fool on all other occasions.

Having had Bungeham as his lodger for the best part of a week, Joe had learned to enjoy his company. Bungeham was full of odd tricks, making coins vanish and reappear from behind Joe's ears, jerking silk handkerchiefs from Joe's pocket when Joe had never known one was there. Such things made Joe's life a series of surprises and puzzled him profoundly. Sometimes he would break off from grooming a horse to make quite he wasn't concealing silk handkerchiefs somewhere about his person.

This Saturday, the pedlar and the ostler went out together with one horse while Dickinson followed with another. It was hard going, reaching some of the isolated farms, and especially difficult coming back again laden.

The farmers were pleased to see someone after seeing only their own families and labourers for several days. But they were not too willing to part with their produce. Like the corn dealers, they had an eye to rising prices and preferred to wait and see what January and February might bring. But few could resist the sight of ready gold. After an attempt at haggling – in which they found the pedlar a master opponent – they agreed to compromise. A bag or two of grain was tossed down from the granary. A few hens, a pig and a sheep were slaughtered.

While Bungeham and the ostler worked to the east of the valley, Dickinson went to the west. They saw him once, a lonely figure on a snowy ridge, leading his horse. As they made their way back in the evening, Bungeham found hoof prints showing that the engineer had preceded them home.

'Joe.'

'Aye?'

'You think I'm an uncommon queer fellow, Joe?'

'Aye.'

'I am uncommon queer,' confirmed Bungeham. 'And it's not at all impossible that I might get uncommon queerer.'

'Oh!'

'If I should get so, please bear with me. If I seem to be telling lies, just agree with me. Nod your head. You can do that, eh?'

'Just as tha says.'

'Because I'm uncommon queer, Joe, it don't mean I'm daft.'

'Nay! Tha's not daft!' agreed Joe, heartily.

It was dark when they reached Penkley. Their way lay past the slatternly little alehouse where Joss Barker had spent much of his time and money. It was frequented by such men as Harthill, Oakes and Simpkins, who found their way there even in the hardest times. Woodrow often called in, too, and if he felt generous bought a penn'orth of ale all round.

When they reached the door of this smoky little den, Bungeham told Joe to wait for him. Joe was rather surprised at this, for the pedlar was a man who usually abstained from strong drink in any form. But Joe was not a person to argue. If Bungeham felt like a drink, let him have one.

Bungeham placed his hand flat on the alehouse door and pushed it open suddenly. In that instant, he was transformed. From the quiet, rather tired fellow who had been leading his horse patiently through the snow, he became a wild, excited man, his eyes staring, his mouth hardly able to frame the words he wished to say.

'Hey!' he gasped, almost falling into the room.

Everyone turned round: Woodrow, smoking a long clay pipe; the man with the beaked nose; Simpkins with the bald head. A dozen astonished faces turned to the door.

'I've seen him!' panted Bungeham. 'Out yonder.'

'Eh?'

'As we were coming along – in Begg's Gully. Joe'll tell you.'

'Saw who?' demanded Woodrow, his pipe falling to the floor and breaking into pieces.

'Hey, Joe!' called Bungeham, opening the door again.

Joe came lumbering in and looked blankly around.

'I stopped you, didn't I, Joe?' the pedlar asked him.

'Oh, aye,' nodded Joe.

'Didn't I point it out? Look there, I said. Right down by the trees. Half covered in snow, wasn't it, Joe?'

Joe followed Bungeham's finger as it pointed along the wall.

'Aye, that's reet.'

Bungeham's finger kept pointing as he continued: 'Could have been a tree trunk with branches spread out, couldn't it, Joe? But it weren't, were it?'

Joe shook his head dutifully.

'No. 'Tweren't,' he confirmed.

'No,' said Bungeham, dropping his finger slowly, and looking from one member of his audience to the next. 'No. It were – a body!'

'*A body?*' someone echoed.

'A lad's body,' said Bungeham. 'You'd say it were a lad's body, wouldn't you, Joe?'

'Eh?' Joe looked just a little uncertain, until he caught Bungeham's eye and added hurriedly, 'Aye – lad's body. No doubt.'

'Well?' demanded Woodrow. 'What have you done about it? Did you go and examine it?'

'What?' exclaimed the pedlar. 'He were right down the gully. Weren't he, Joe?'

'Reet down.' Joe now stood peering into the depths as the pedlar's finger directed him.

'You're sure it was a lad?' asked Woodrow.

'Sure of it!'

Woodrow turned to the others.

'It must be young Tankard. Down Begg's Gully, of all places!'

'Ee!' smirked Harthill. 'This'll break yon mill owner.'

'Then you go and tell 'im,' said Woodrow. 'See how he takes it.'

The others, having overcome their surprise, now wished to interrogate the pedlar more closely.

'Which way didst tha come back past t' Gully?' someone asked.

'From Appleby's farm. Appleby's farm, weren't it, Joe?'

Joe nodded.

'I must go and tell 'em at Packhorse,' said Bungeham, anxious to break away from his questioners. 'Mr Dickinson's waiting for us up yon.'

They managed to get out, and as they trudged off towards the inn, Bungeham noticed Woodrow slipping across the road towards his shop.

'Ee!' said Joe, half admiringly. 'Tha's a reet queer 'un, Abel Bungeham! Tha's playing more tricks now than gettin' pennies out of ear'oles!'

'Aye,' said Bungeham, imitating the dialect, 'tha's reet there, lad!'

They came within sight of the Packhorse.

'What did tha mean by all yon?' asked Joe.

'You'll see in good time. I'm just stirring things up a little. All I ask of you, Joe, is that you back me up. Don't let 'em know I'm fibbing.'

'Not if tha says so. Though, dang me, I don't know what tha's up to!'

'You will.'

'Art telling same yarn to Mr Dickinson?' asked Joe.

But before he had a reply, a bugle note came echoing among the silent houses, and Bungeham stopped and held up his hand.

'The coach! Here's the coach, Joe! I'm in luck! I'm in luck!'

'Aye. Two days late – but it's come at last.'

The ostler slapped the weary horse on its flank, and they ran together in great excitement down to the inn.

Dickinson was already in the yard. He had stabled his horse and piled all his purchases in an empty outbuilding.

'The coach is coming!' shouted Joe. 'She's just down t' road!'

Hurriedly, he unloosed the burden from the horse, and while Bungeham humped the carcases away, he led the beast to its stall. A few minutes later, the mud-spattered Clevelands turned into the yard, dragging the heavy coach behind them. At once, Bassenthwaite and Dickinson went forward to catch their bridles, while Bungeham, emerging from the outbuilding, fixed his eye on a slight figure wrapped up in rugs almost to suffocation who was huddled inside in the corner.

As Bassenthwaite handed the other passengers down – there were two middle-aged men and a young woman – Bungeham bustled out their companion, and before anyone noticed, had conveyed him to the stables, screened from view by the coach and its team of four.

'What's happened to the lad?' asked the young woman, turning round.

The two men, spying ahead of them the blazing fire in the taproom, took no heed of her words, and Bassenthwaite was busy with the luggage. But Dickinson had heard what she said, and looked across the yard just as Bungeham disappeared from view. He decided to wait in the doorway until the pedlar came out again.

Meanwhile Bungeham was urging the boy up the ladder to the loft. Having lodged him there, he slipped quietly down again, leaving the boy trying to warm his hands by rubbing them vigorously together.

The coach, with its horses taken out, still stood in the yard, but there was a little group in front of the inn door which had not been there earlier. Two of Tankard's men were confronting Dickinson.

'What's this?' he was asking them.

'Are you coming without trouble?' The tone was harsh and threatening.

'You must give me good reason why I should.'

'Because you are under arrest, John Dickinson.'

'What? Again? Is this a weekly occurrence?'

'We have a warrant. Show it to him, Bob.'

One of the men pulled a paper from the breast of his coat.

'Keep it,' said Dickinson. 'I can answer any charge. You know that, Bungeham.'

'It depends what the charge is,' said Bungeham.

'This is a charge of murder,' said one of the constables.

'Murder!' sneered Dickinson. 'You tell them, Bungeham.'

'I've told them,' replied the pedlar, winking over the men's heads.

Dickinson frowned and kept his eyes on the ragged figure.

'Aye,' said the constable, turning to Bungeham. 'And I must warn thee also. Tha must stay here where we can send for thee.'

Dickinson stood there looking hard at the pedlar. Only when the pedlar winked again and placed his finger to his lips did he give the slightest nod.

'Right,' he said, turning to the constables. 'I'll come.'

When he had been escorted away, Bungeham slipped from the knot of onlookers and returned to the stable loft.

'We've a lot to tell each other,' he said to Jeremy. 'And I've a lot of explaining to do.'

*

Meanwhile, the apothecary hurried back to his shop and burst in through the door.

'Sam! Sam!'

The lad was busy eating in the kitchen, and brought his plate with him when he answered the summons. Woodrow was already searching through the drawers behind the counter.

'Where's Begg's Gully?' he demanded.

'Begg's Gully! Why, it be a couple o' mile off – ower yon, afore tha gets to Appleby's. A reet place. Banks like that!' He inclined his arm to indicate the slope. 'And watter at bottom.'

'Get your coat on, then. And your hat and mitts – all them things I gave you.'

'I'm not going theer!' declared Sam stubbornly.

'En't you? I says you are. But before you wrap yourself up, I'd like to see you over here. And you can slip that jacket off.'

'Eh? What for?'

Having found what he was looking for in the drawer, the apothecary faced around. Sam's eyes fastened on the lancet in his hands.

'What's that?' he asked, backing away.

'Come here,' ordered his employer, 'and get that sleeve rolled up.'

'No! Keep off me! Don't tha dare touch me!'

'Stop snivelling. Hold your sleeve up. I'm not going to kill you.'

Suddenly he snatched hold of the boy by the arm and pulled him roughly towards him.

'Don't touch me!' screamed the lad as the instrument gleamed in the light.

'Be quiet and hold your noise!'

The boy trembled violently as Woodrow pushed up his ragged shirtsleeve. But he seemed powerless to do anything more than protest.

'Here! Hold this bowl. Keep it steady now.'

'Oh, no!' gasped Sam, in an agony of apprehension. 'Ouch! Tha's hurt me! Ouch!'

'Keep still, you little fool!'

The blood dripped out of the vein. The apothecary let it flow for a little while as Sam stared at his wounded arm, his face tensed, his teeth chattering with fear.

'There we are!' Woodrow placed the bowl on the counter and took a strip of linen from the drawer. 'I'll bind it up. You'll be all the better for it... not feel a thing.'

Sam looked ghastly, however.

'Come on!' urged the apothecary, trying to humour him. 'I thought you were a man. I've seen braver girls.'

He finished binding the wound, and then pulled the sleeve down again, saying, 'Here! Have a drink of this.'

He offered the lad a flask of brandy. Sam smelled it and took a gulp. Not being used to neat spirits, he began to choke. When he had recovered, Woodrow looked at him and laughed, mockingly.

'You're a fine 'un, hinney!'

Then despite Sam's protests he compelled him to don his outer garments.

'Now, listen,' he said when the boy was ready. 'Take this spanner. Maybe you've seen one like it. And this phial – it's full of your own blood. Get off to Begg's Gully as hard as you can. Keep to the road where folk have churned up the snow.'

'Aye – an' what then?'

'There's a body in the Gully – young Tankard's. Don't ask me how it got there. I don't know. But there it is. Make it look as though he died from a spanner, and leave the spanner lying somewhere near.'

'Like I did wi' t' stick?'

'The same. Only this time, take more care. Don't be seen! Tankard'll be out there himself, I've no doubt. You might even meet him. See that no one sees you, either going down the Gully or coming out.'

'What do I get for doing all this?' asked Sam as he pocketed the tool and the phial.

'If it's done fast and done proper, it's worth a golden guinea, lad.'

'I'll do it,' said Sam.

He gave a grin – the first for some time – and went out into the night, while Woodrow laughed to himself.

Fourteen: Treason has done his worst

Joe the ostler was the best of fellows for getting food, so Jeremy and Bungeham were able to enjoy a far better meal in the stable loft than the guests were having across the yard.

As they ate, they talked.

'And the Old Complaint?' asked Jeremy. 'Was there never really an Old Complaint at all?'

'There was indeed,' declared the actor, for Bungeham and Dempsey were one and the same. 'And a terrible complaint it was. I had the bottle by the throat so often that it had me by the throat, too. It spoiled my acting. It emptied my pockets. It played the very devil with me. Finally it landed me in the Marshalsea for debt. And there – well, I won't say I couldn't have continued drinking, because men drink almost as heavily in there as they do outside – but by making a tremendous effort, I stopped. And I haven't touched a drop since.'

'But Mrs Heller said—'

'Never mind what Mrs Heller said,' smiled Dempsey. 'Whatever she may think or say, she's been wrong. I've used the Old Complaint as an excuse several times, but the Old Complaint has never been a reason. I wanted to do something which only an actor could do – a bit of acting off the stage.'

'That's what you've been doing here?'

Dempsey nodded. 'And now the play is nearly done. Our villainous spy has worked for Dickinson's downfall—'

'And poor Caleb! Was he badly hurt?'

'Luckily, no! But see what they planned for you!'

'That boy Sam! Why should he hate me so much?'

'He was a warped soul. He began by hating your uncle, so he naturally hates your uncle's nephew.'

'But why involve Mr Dickinson?'

'It's the result of a bad system. Woodrow gets a bounty for

133

every felon condemned through his informing. He had one bounty on Barker. He hopes for another on Dickinson. But he not only gets rewarded in this way by the Government, he gets another income from your uncle. It pays him to stir up trouble, and he's one of those people who just loves mischief.'

'And what about your present plans?'

'Well, Jeremy, I'm sure our informer friend will have to interfere in some way. But he can't succeed, whatever he tries. So we must wait now, and hold our cards to our chest.'

*

Meanwhile, Sam was floundering along as fast as he could through the snow. Despite the cold, it was warm work. The night was dark and no one was in sight.

It took him some time to reach Begg's Gully, and when he saw it he found it so steep that he hesitated to slide down its side. Instead he went some way along the edge before descending at a point where a number of stunted trees and bushes made the going easier.

The snow reflected a faint light and he made his way along by the frozen watercourse at the bottom, searching from left to right as he went. There was no sign of anything beyond a few rocks and boulders. As he proceeded, the sides grew steeper until he found himself in a narrow little gully within the main gully, and he was moving warily along it when suddenly he heard voices far above. A light showed like a pinpoint high up the slope. Sam stood breathless and watched. 'Let no one see you,' Woodrow had said. 'It's worth a golden guinea.' The thought of the guinea made him determined to remain hidden.

'Eh, Will!' called one of the men above. 'Mind tha footin', it's slippery ower here.'

'I'm goin' no further,' said the other. 'Wait till daylight, I say.'

'Tha tell Tankard, then. Tell him tha daresn't go down.'

The light bobbed about, coming lower.

'Watch out, Will! Tha nearly had me head ower tip.'

'I'm goin' no farther. Tha can break thy neck if tha wants.'

They were about fifty feet up, and by this time Sam was

134

terrified. He knew they could not reach him: no one could descend those last twenty feet without injury. But they might see him standing there, and at all costs he wished to prevent that.

So he made a desperate decision, and flung himself face down in the snow, lying absolutely still, like a corpse.

He could still hear the men descending, and by now lumps of ice and snow pattered down about him.

'Look!' he heard one of them shout. 'That's 'im! Down theer.'

Suddenly, something muffled hurtled down. There was the crash of glass and the clang of metal. The lamp shattered on a rock.

'Dang thee! Tha fool – look what tha's done!'

'I'm going back up – if I can climb up.'

'That's 'im, though. Down theer!'

'Aye, but we'll fetch 'im up in t' morning. If Tankard wants 'im tonight, he can fetch him hisself. Danged if I'm riskin' me neck!'

When it was clear that the men were climbing painfully up to the top again, Sam breathed again with relief. After a while he could see them no more, he pulled himself out of the snow.

For a little while he continued his own search, but without success. Finally, he took out the phial, sprinkled the spanner with blood and tossed it into the snow near to where he had lain. The rest of the contents he scattered around, and then he too returned to Penkley, resolved not to say a word about what had actually happened.

*

Tankard's men arrived at the Gable House late that night, and found Dickinson held in custody in the passage. They were told to go straight through into the magistrate's room.

'Well?' asked the mill owner, looking up sullenly. 'Hast tha brought him? Was it my lad?'

'He's at the bottom o' yon gully, reet enough.'

'But we couldn't get down to 'im. Happen in t' morning—'

'I sent thee to fetch him back!' thundered Tankard. 'Tha's been long enough out there – near four hours, I reckon.'

'It's too bad out there, Mr Tankard. There's no footing. We lost the lamp, as it was. We weren't going to risk our necks.'

'No, tha weren't!' agreed the mill owner sarcastically. 'But let's have the prisoner in.'

Dickinson came in defiantly, angrily shaking off the grip of one of the constables who tried to lead him by the arm.

'Now listen, Dickinson.' Tankard wagged a magisterial finger at him. 'I'll hear this case fully in the morning. Tonight I'm keeping you locked up.'

'You'll hear what case?' demanded Dickinson. 'What am I being charged with?'

'With murder – as you know full well.'

'Nonsense.'

'Are you addressing the Bench?'

'I'm telling you the charge is nonsense. If I am charged with murder, Your Worship, may I enquire whose murder?'

Tankard went red with anger at being addressed with such calculated insolence.

'You know dang well,' he retorted. 'My nephew.'

'Nonsense,' repeated Dickinson.

'Oh, it's nonsense, is it? Let me tell you, Mr Dickinson, this time we've seen the body.'

'That's utterly impossible.'

'Maybe you think so, having thrown the lad's body into Begg's Gully. But my men have seen him.'

Dickinson stared. The colour drained from his face.

'Who's seen him?'

'Will Turner here, for one.'

'Impossible. It must be someone else!'

'Ho, ho! So it must be someone else? Tha knows it must be someone else, eh? Tha's tying thy own noose very nicely, Mr Dickinson.'

Tankard turned to his officers. 'Take him away. And get down that gully first thing tomorrow. We'll get evidence even Mr Dickinson won't deny.'

*

One by one the last lights of Penkley were snuffed out. Sleep did not come so easily. The townsfolk knew they were perched on the brink of some great climax. So much was to be done on the morrow. For, although Caleb could not sleep for thinking of the signal he must give, the word had already gone abroad. Weapons were to hand, knives sharpened, hammers, pitchforks, scythe blades, all in readiness. Their owners could hardly sleep, and longed for daylight. So did Jeremy and Dempsey in their mouse-ridden loft. So did Dickinson in his damp cell, and Reuben Tankard, mourning his lost heir and dead ambitions in the Gable House. Morning could not come too soon.

Dempsey and the ostler had breakfast together in the kitchen. Neither mentioned Jeremy, who remained out of sight in the loft. How Joe succeeded in getting a second rasher of gammon from Bessie, only Joe could say, but Jeremy ate the rasher with appetite.

'By the way,' he told Dempsey when the actor rejoined him. 'I saw a number of dragoons collecting up Bolton way.'

'Dragoons?'

'A sergeant was waiting for them to assemble at the posting house. They'd been billeted in various alehouses and taverns round the district, and from what I could make out, were slow at coming up.'

'When was this?'

'Yesterday afternoon. I was wondering if there'd been trouble over that way.'

'Not that I know of.'

But plainly, Dempsey was worried by the intelligence, and he sat frowning while the sound of the church bell echoed across the frozen town.

'I went to church last Sunday,' he said, 'and though I'd like to go today, I'm afraid I'll have to remain here.'

Meanwhile the congregation was gathering, and as the people arrived, rumour buzzed around the church. Then suddenly it was silenced with, 'Hush! Here's parson.'

It was plain that Mr Openshaw was ill. His face was white, his eyes sunken and bloodshot. He swayed as he stood.

'When the wicked man turneth away from the wickedness which he hath committed…'

So, in the customary way, the service began.

'Where's Woodrow?' whispered Jess Harthill to his neighbour as the minister pronounced the absolution.

'Haven't seen him. We'll miss him at singing.'

'A good fellow, Woodrow. Cured me of the ague. Knows how to treat illnesses better than any fancy physician.'

Had they known, the apothecary was at that moment walking into the inn yard carrying a small bundle under his arm. And it so happened that Joe was then leading one of the wheelers – a big handsome roan, young and rather high-spirited – round the yard for a little exercise.

'Hello, Joe.'

'Mornin', Mr Woodrow.'

In the loft, Dempsey (who had been lying down) sat up immediately.

'Things are stirring,' he whispered to Jeremy. 'Quick! Pass me my pedlar's bag.'

From the bottom of the bag he produced two pistols, examined their priming, and slid one into each of the pockets of his coat. He then descended the ladder.

'I want to hire a horse rather urgently,' Woodrow was explaining to the ostler as Dempsey appeared.

Woodrow looked round to see who had come out of the stables.

'Ah! My friend Bungeham! How are you today? That was a terrible discovery you made yesterday.'

'Aye,' grumbled the pedlar, 'and likely to keep me here as witness against my will, when I've a whole bag o' trinkets and laces and fancy stuff to dispose of. I can't keep body and soul together if I can't get about and sell my goods! I've learned my lesson, though. I should ha' minded my own business.'

The apothecary was not in the least interested in the complaints of a pedlar. He was anxious to be on his way.

'Come!' he urged, turning to Joe. 'Is there a good horse I can hire?'

The ostler was about to reply when the pedlar interrupted.

'I didn't tell you what else I found up by Begg's Gully.'

'Eh?' asked Woodrow, turning round. 'What else did you find?'

'A stick.'

'A stick?' The apothecary's eyes narrowed. 'What sort of a stick?'

'Well, Joe says it's a crab apple stick.'

'Does he now?'

'I threw it in yonder outhouse. Would you like to see it?'

'Why! Aye!'

'Then come over here. I'll show you.'

The bewildered ostler blinked, and then, as the horse he was holding shook its head violently, he seemed to divine that this was a continuation of the previous piece of play-acting, and led the animal back to the stable.

'It's in here,' said the pedlar.

Dempsey opened a creaking weather-worn door and indicated a filthy interior where roosters had previously found a home among the straw.

'In here?' asked Woodrow, going in and looking around. 'Whereabouts?'

'Isn't it over there in the corner?'

'I don't see it.'

'No?'

Dempsey stood in the doorway blocking the light.

'Don't move,' he said in a crisp, authoritative voice.

Woodrow spun round. The sunlight glinted on the barrel of the pistol in the actor's hand.

'What do you mean by this?' Woodrow's tremulous accents betrayed his terror.

'The game's up, Mr Woodrow – or should I call you Mr Hardisty Catchpole? If you raise your voice or try to attack me, I'll have no hesitation in shooting you like a dog.'

'What do you mean?' stammered Woodrow. 'Who are you? What is all this?'

'Don't try and excuse yourself. If you thought you could get out of Penkley till the trouble's over, you've made a nasty mistake. Things aren't going so well for you this time. This isn't Nottingham.'

'Nottingham? What d'you know of Nottingham?'

'Enough. You had a rich haul there, Mr Catchpole. But it'll only be a poor one here.'

The informer stared about him for some means of reversing his position, but Dempsey waved the pistol at him.

'Don't try it. I'm a very good shot.'

At this moment Joe returned from the stable and, seeing Dempsey in the doorway, came to see what was happening.

'Hast found t' stick?' he asked.

'Joe!' pleaded the apothecary. 'This ruffian is threatening me.'

'Aye,' confirmed Joe, looking at the pistol, 'so he is.'

'There's another in this left-hand pocket,' said Dempsey to the ostler. 'Pull it out and keep him covered.'

'Aye,' said Joe. 'Reet.'

And he did exactly as he was told.

'Keep him quiet,' ordered Dempsey. 'Shoot him dead if he moves a step.'

Joe nodded, and the actor pocketed his own pistol and hurried up to the loft to consult Jeremy. A few minutes later, he and the boy came down into the yard and confronted the terrified informer.

'Young Tankard!' gasped the man. 'How came you here?'

'Never mind,' snapped Dempsey. 'Not from any care of yours, we might be certain.'

He turned to Joe and spoke in a low voice.

'I want you to get along to the Gable House, and if at all possible, without being seen. I don't think it'll be too hard on a Sunday morning, but don't go down the main streets, just the same. Take Jeremy and this – vermin – with you. Then wait in the old wash house across the yard until I call for you. It may be a little while. But don't worry… and be wary.'

He turned to Jeremy.

'Take my other pistol, lad. And good luck!'

He looked across the inn yard. The empty coach screened the doorway from the opposite windows. No one was about.

'Come on, Mr Catchpole,' he called to the spy. 'Keep a pace or two ahead of Joe, and go wherever he says. And if you want to keep alive, don't do anything silly.'

There was a gap in the fencing by the stable. Dempsey watched the three figures going through, and confident that Joe would fulfil whatever duties were laid upon him, he went back to the stable loft to await Tankard's summons.

*

Meanwhile, the church service was dragging along. There was a greater restlessness than ever, a continual whispering and shuffling of feet. The vicar was almost inaudible. His sermon was incoherent. He lost his way in it completely and came to an agonising halt. Then he fumbled for a fresh start, found it impossible to regain the thread of his discourse, and brought it to an end with a heartfelt 'Let us pray'.

The hymn which followed was thunderous. At long last, the battle cry was raised. Its original purpose as a signal had been frustrated, but it made a tremendous emotional appeal. The parishioners sang as they had never sung, the glint of battle in their eyes. All thoughts of peace and love and Christian pilgrimage fled from their minds.

> 'One here will constant be,
> Come wind, come weather;
> There's no discouragement
> Shall make him once relent...'

Fierce determination echoed in the words, for the wind and weather were the wind and weather of that bleak December day. The discouragements were all to be found in Penkley. The valour was their own, and they were the ones who would never relent against the harsh masters who governed their lives.

No wonder they sang with such ferocity and never noticed the man in the threadbare cassock, who remained on his knees throughout the hymn.

Somehow, at the end, the vicar struggled to his feet and managed to totter into the chancel to pronounce the blessing.

'...Be upon you, and remain with you, evermore.'

But the congregation yearned to leave. As their pastor crumpled up and toppled in a heap down the chancel steps, they poured out of the building.

'Father!' cried Caleb, darting forward.

Old Kinch was the only other person to notice. Together they raised the fallen man's head.

'Water,' said Caleb. 'Get him some water. And fetch Woodrow.'

Fifteen: In the presence of dread justice

Reuben Tankard looked angrily at the men who stood before him.

'What are you telling me?' he demanded. 'The body's *gone*?'

'It were theer last neet,' declared Will. 'Weren't it, Robbie?'

'It were that! I seed it mesel'. Yet there were nowt theer this morning.'

'Nobbut yon spanner,' added Will.

Tankard picked the spanner up from the table. 'And they left this, did they?'

He held it carefully between his fingers, and looked at the stains upon it.

'Aye, it's bloody,' commented Will. 'There were blood all over the place.'

'Great black drops on t' snow,' said Robbie.

'What about footprints?' asked the mill owner.

'Now, we looked for them careful, didn't we, Will?'

'Aye. There were nowt but one set, comin' and goin'.'

'One set? One man had walked there, and walked back?'

'That's as it were.'

'You followed the trail?'

'Aye. Reckon he'd slid down by t'copse.'

'That's reet, Mr Tankard.'

'And how had he left?'

'Reet along t' gully and up t' bank.'

Tankard considered the matter, still holding the spanner and examining it attentively.

'Must ha' been a big man,' he remarked.

'Maybe. But his boots weren't ower big.'

'Must ha' been a strong man, then, to carry yon lad all that way.' He considered the matter again.

'There were more than one o' them in this,' he declared at length.

'Happen there were,' said Will.

'A conspiracy to murder my boy,' ruminated the mill owner. 'To murder him and hide the body.'

'Aye. If it had snowed again we might never ha' found him till springtime,' said Robbie.

'Dickinson's behind this,' declared Tankard. 'I know it! I've been told it on good authority. He murdered my lad last Saturday week and, later on, threw his body in t' gully.'

'What about t' blood?' asked Will. 'Tha's thinkin' t' lad were murdered in t' churchyard.'

'And he were, too,' snapped Tankard.

'But t' blood's on t' snow in t' gully. And that's where we found t' spanner.'

'Aye,' muttered the mill owner. 'There's summat here as don't fit. But I tell thee, Dickinson was out after that lad to kill him. And kill him he did. Isn't this his spanner?'

'Aye. That's John Dickinson's.'

Another of Tankard's men came in.

'Ah! Blackburn! Hast fetched pedlar fellow?'

'He's in t' passage.'

'Good! You told t' parson also, didst tha? I want him at all costs. Dismiss the case, would he? I'll show him the sort of case it was he wanted dismissing!'

'Sorry. But t' parson's been took bad. They're fetching Woodrow to him.'

'Took bad? He can't take bad. There's a case here he's got to listen to. Go and tell him I want him urgent.'

'He's reet bad, Mr Tankard. He's white as a sheet.'

'Go and fetch him just the same. Parsons have plenty of time to get well again. They never do no real sort o' work.'

Blackburn opened his mouth to protest even more cogently, but the mill owner's glance brooked no argument. The man took his hat and went.

'Now,' said Tankard, 'let's have yon pedlar in. Better get pen and paper ready. We can take his deposition before t' parson comes. It'll save time.'

Dempsey was ushered in unceremoniously. Tankard's constables had little respect for pedlars. The sooner pedlars were hustled over the parish bounds the better, from their point of view.

The mill owner placed the spanner on the table again as the actor was pushed violently into the middle of the room.

'What's tha name?' he demanded gruffly.

'Abel Bungeham, Y' Worship.'

'Aye! And what are you?'

'I'm a pedlar, Y'Worship. An honest man, sir. I travel up and down the country, sir. They know me from Carlisle to Cannock Chase.'

'Aye. Well, tha can tell that in the alehouse. I've more important things to ask thee.'

'About last night, no doubt?'

'About last night,' nodded the magistrate.

The actor wet his lips like a man who is extremely nervous. He glanced at Will, who was ready, pen in hand, to scribble down the deposition.

'Why are you examining me?' he asked, seemingly terror-stricken. 'You en't accusing me of nothing, are you? I never done a thing. I swear!'

'We're not accusing thee of anything, tha fool!' rapped out Tankard.

The actor gave a deep sigh of relief. 'Then what's he a-writin' of?' he enquired.

'Sithee, man,' snapped Tankard, losing his patience. 'I'm asking t' questions, not thee!'

'But if I'm not accused—' began Dempsey innocently.

'No. Tha's not accused. Have I told thee tha was?'

'Then, if I'm not accused, Y'Worship – who is?'

'Never thee mind. It's nowt to do with thee.'

'No?' returned Dempsey. 'Then I'll say good day.'

'You'll stay where you are!' ordered the magistrate. 'Do you have no respect for the Bench?'

'Oh, yes, Y'Worship.'

'I sent for thee to give evidence.'

'But I can't give evidence,' protested Dempsey.

Tankard glared at him. His original impression that the pedlar was a stupid bumpkin was fast being dispelled.

'And why not?' he asked.

'I'm not under oath.'

'Tha will be, once parson arrives. He'll conduct this hearing.'

'Then why ask me questions now?'

The mill owner glowered at the man at the other side of the table. Dempsey stood in front of him, the picture of innocence, his expression all the more irritating to Tankard for being devoid of all rancour, cunning or dissimulation.

'Bring the prisoner in,' ordered the mill owner after a moment or two of thought.

Dickinson was led in after a short delay. He was unshaven and dirty. His clothes were creased from having been slept in. He cast a surly glance at Tankard.

'John Dickinson,' said the magistrate in a deep pontifical voice, 'you are accused of the murder of Jeremy Tankard. Have you anything to say?'

Dickinson cleared his throat, and a hush fell on the room while they awaited his reply. It was then that a distant discord was heard – indistinct and indefinable, but loud enough to make the magistrate look up and tilt his head to hear better.

'It's a lie,' said Dickinson, as if he had not heard the sound.

'A lie, is it?' returned Tankard, picking up the spanner. 'Do you know what this it?'

The noise was coming nearer. It swelled and retreated as the wind blew.

'And whose it is?' continued the mill owner.

'Like as not,' growled Dickinson, 'it's mine.'

'Like as not,' Tankard turned to his scribe. 'Are you noting the answers, Will?'

'Yes, Y'Worship.'

The sound grew louder. Was it a song? Were the people singing in Penkley on this bitter day?

'Last night a body was seen lying at the foot of Begg's Gully,' Tankard went on, using the spanner to emphasis his points. 'Robbie Wilson here can give evidence of it. Speak up, Robbie.'

'Aye, Y'Worship. I seed a body reet enough. Me and Will seed it, plain as plain.'

'Was it a boy's body?'

'It were a boy, sir. I'd say it were a boy. What about thee, Will?'

Will looked up from scratching on the paper and nodded.

'And this man here,' continued Tankard, pointing the spanner at Dempsey, 'will say that he saw a body there yesterday afternoon.'

There was certainly singing in Penkley streets – raucous singing. A hymn, strangely interspersed with whoops and shouts.

'Well?' asked Tankard. 'Didn't you?'

Dempsey had remained silent. Now he gave a start, as though he had awakened from a reverie.

'I said I thought I saw a body.'

'*Thought!* You did see it, you fool! And these men saw it also.'

'If I did – and if they did—'

'What do you mean by "if they did"? They've declared they did.'

Dempsey ignored the interruption.

'If they did,' he went on, 'they didn't see Jeremy Blatchford's body.'

'What are you talking about? How do you know?'

'They couldn't have seen it, because this charge of murdering Jeremy Blatchford is complete nonsense.'

The magistrate stared at him, dumbfounded.

'What are you talking about?' he repeated.

'Nothing I can't prove,' said Dempsey with calm superiority. 'If you'll excuse me for one moment…'

And he had slipped out of the room before anyone could intervene.

'Why didn't you stop him?' demanded Tankard of his minions. 'And who's making all that hubbub out there? Have a look, Robbie.'

The next moment Dempsey was back. He closed the door behind him but retained hold of the knob.

'There can be no charge of murdering Jeremy Blatchford, Your Worship,' he said quietly, 'for Jeremy Blatchford has yet to be murdered.'

At this cue, Jeremy entered the room, closely followed by Woodrow, with Joe the ostler at his heels holding a pistol against the small of the apothecary's back. The mill owner was so astounded at the entrance of this little procession that he let the spanner fall from his hands, and it crashed on to the table, upsetting the ink all over Will's sheets of paper.

'Jeremy! I never thought to see thee again, lad.'

'If he had been murdered,' said Dempsey, pushing the abject figure of the spy up to the table, 'this wretch would have been the man responsible! This is the man who has done nothing but plot and plan ever since – at your invitation, don't forget, Mr Tankard – he arrived here. As you must admit, Mr Tankard, he has been secretly sending you information, accusing Joss Barker of sedition, and generally sowing trouble and discord.' He pointed dramatically out of the window. 'Why are these men marching upon us, do you suppose? Only because this man has instigated them. But what they don't know, and what I myself have only just found out, is that this traitor – this damnable smiling villain – has also arranged for them to test their strength with the King's Dragoons.'

'Dragoons?' asked the bewildered magistrate. 'What dragoons? Who has sent for dragoons?'

'You'll be glad I have done,' whined the spy. 'You'll be glad of my foresight – for you'll be needing them.'

The townsfolk in procession had ceased their singing now, and were running up to the Gable House, shouting and throwing stones.

Robbie, breathless, dashed into the room.

'They've gone mad!' he panted. 'There's that young Sam in t' front, urgin' 'em on. And Harthill and Simpkins, and all the ringleaders!'

'I told thee there'd be trouble,' said Dickinson angrily to the mill owner.

'Aye! And tha caused it,' retorted Tankard.

'Oh, no!' argued Dempsey. 'This little whining wretch caused it, Mr Tankard. And you yourself.'

A volley of stones crashed against the front shutters. The remainder of the unprotected fanlight shattered into splinters. Old Martha came scuttling in, terrified, and clung to Robbie. Tankard stood up, resolute.

'Keep a close watch on this man.' He indicated the spy. 'I'll deal with him in good time.'

'And where are you going?' asked Dempsey.

'To the door.'

'No, no! That's asking for trouble. They're not in a pleasant mood.'

This was an understatement. Shouts of, 'Tankard! Come outside, Tankard! Let's hang Tankard! Where's a gallows for Tankard?' were already echoing around the houses.

It was useless for moderate men like Matthew Oakes and Will Hampson to try to restrain the enthusiasm of the mob they had called out. Many of the workers of Penkley had been unemployed for weeks. They were hungry and angry. Above all, they were bored and dispirited. The excitement of mob action went to their heads. Being denied any creative work, they felt an irresistible urge to destroy. So Oakes and Hampson were jeered when they pleaded for discipline. Wilder men took charge. Harthill and Simpkins became the heroes, and out in front marched a new leader – young Sam, his ragged coat bulging with strange missiles, a huge cleaver brandished in one hand and a knife in the other.

'Fight for the Rights of Man!' yelled Harthill. 'Don't let yourselves be slaves for ever!'

The mob, swollen by every able-bodied person from the foetid streets, including women with babes in their arms, children, and white-haired old men, surged down to the Gable House. Enthusiasm for the Rights of Men soared high. But out in front, young Sam was not interested in rights of any sort.

'Smash 'em up!' he roared, hurling a half-brick through an innocent window.

This appealed to the instincts of youth. Everyone searched for missiles. Cobblestones were prised up. Shutters were ripped down. The concerted strength of ten lads pushed the coping off walls. Curtains were torn off their rods. Barrels of apples spilled over the road. People scrambled and fought among themselves for whatever booty was discovered, but the march on the Gable House continued.

'Tankard! We want Tankard!'

'Hang Tankard.'

'Tankard to the gallows!'

'Release John Dickinson – or you'll die for it, Tankard!'

Stones rattled against the Gable House and ricocheted from the brickwork. Then, in the midst of the volleys, the door was seen to open. It moved about an inch, but as stones were thudding against it, whoever had unbolted it, dared not open it further.

'Stop! Stop!' yelled Matthew Oakes, hoarse from repeatedly trying to restore order.

The volley could not be kept up for long because no more stones were available. As it ceased, the door of the house was swung right back.

'Tankard!' went up the cry. Then it died. For it was not Tankard on the doorstep, but John Dickinson.

'Fools!' he shouted. 'Get back to your homes at once.'

'We want Tankard! We want Tankard!' chanted the mob.

'Listen to me,' yelled Dickinson. 'You've been betrayed. There are dragoons coming to Penkley!'

'Let 'em come,' shouted back young Sam. 'We'll fight any dragoons. See if we don't.' And he waved his cleaver above his head.

Others behind him who bore knives and scythes also seemed to relish the idea.

'Don't be dang fools!' Dickinson told them. 'We've all been fools enough already.'

But young Sam turned to face the mob at his back.

'Are we going back without Tankard?' he asked.

'Not us! We've come for t' mill owner. We've come to string him up.'

'Then you'd hang the wrong man!' shouted Dickinson. 'For here's the man who's betrayed us all. This is the man we thought our friend.'

Dempsey, who was in the passage behind Dickinson, pushed forward the frightened apothecary.

'Aha!' yelled Sam, laughing hysterically and pointing a mocking finger at his late master. 'So they've caught thee? Aha! Tha was just a bit too clever, Mr Woodrow!'

'Don't be so sure, you little fool!' snarled Woodrow.

Sam came forward to the foot of the steps, still laughing.

'I'll tell 'em all they wants to know about thee, Mr Woodrow.'

'Tha'll tell 'em nowt!'

'I will. I'm the leader now. I'm t' man these lads listen to.' He looked up at Dickinson. 'And tha'll listen to me as well, Mr Dickinson. Unless tha wants tha head split open.'

He waved his cleaver menacingly.

'And this is what I thinks o' t' Gable House,' went on Sam, producing a bottle from his pocket.

'Don't be a dang fool!'

It was Tankard who had come forward, and as they saw him, the mob gave a great deafening shout. Then things happened in violent succession. With a wild whoop, Sam flung the bottle through the upper window of the house. With glass flying in fragments, it burst into flame even as it vanished from view. At the same time, the apothecary leapt down the steps, seized the lad's arm and tried to wrest the cleaver from his grasp.

'*Hold it!*' shouted Dempsey coming after him and brandishing the pistol.

He had hardly reached the pair when there was a dreadful yell. The spy staggered back a pace and collapsed, bleeding from a terrible wound to the head. Sam, with the glint of murder in his eyes, shouted for support and charged up to the door. His bloodstained weapon dripped as he swung it.

Dempsey was borne back in the rush. There was a confused struggle in the porch. Suddenly, above the shouts and oaths came the sharp report of a pistol. The lad spun round, mortally wounded, and letting the cleaver clatter down on the stones, he tottered and fell on top of the man he had just killed.

There was a shocked silence. Everyone stared at the two bodies and the widening pool of blood in which they lay. Then, the silence was broken with a cry of panic.

'*Cavalry!*'

'*Dragoons!*'

Two or three horsemen had come up behind the crowd and were spurring their mounts up the narrow way. Their cloaks were flung back, their heavy sabres raised for action.

'Get off the road!' Shouts and screams of panic went up. 'Get out of the way!'

More horsemen appeared. Those at the rear began to seek

ways to escape. Women tried to find refuge in houses. Their shrieking children clung to their skirts, terrified at the sight of the tall dragoons with their sword blades shining coldly, full of menace. A chorus of shouts from those at the head of the mob urged those behind to stop pressing, but to face about and stand their ground.

To add to the fear and confusion, flames suddenly licked out of the windows of the upper storey of the Gable House. There was an ominous crackle of woodwork burning, sparks danced out over the heads of the crowd, and a curl of smoke grew thicker and blacker.

'Quick!' Dempsey turned to Tankard. 'Use your authority as a magistrate. Tell the crowd to disperse, and order the military to withdraw.'

At the sight of the burning house and the armed mob outside it, the soldiers had halted. But many of the young rioters, finding escape impossible as the road was blocked by the dragoons at one end and their own fellow marchers at the other, were already turning with the courage of desperation to face their assailants. Harthill was boldly urging them to do so rather than be trampled down.

'Read the Riot Act,' Dempsey urged the hesitant magistrate.

Dickinson, on the other hand, was more concerned with the safety of his fellow citizens. He was anxious to prevail upon the militant head of the last procession to forget their grievances and flee. Only thus could their followers get away from the trap.

'Clear the road,' he shouted. 'Get home! All of you!'

Overhead the timbers were crackling viciously, shooting sparks out like gunfire. Smoke drifted down the staircase in thick clouds. Jeremy and Martha, who had been out of view in the passage, were compelled to seek fresh air.

The leading cavalrymen were uncertain whether to attack or not, and came cantering up towards the rear of the crowd in a half-hearted way.

'Strike them down!' yelled Harthill. 'Pull up the cobbles!'

The dragoons halted, and gave the crowd the opportunity to prove hostile. But before any missile could be thrown, or any decisive action taken, an ungainly figure in a black cassock emerged from a narrow passage further down the street and plunged amidst the mass of cavalrymen, pulling at their boots and stirrups.

'Stop! Stop!' he implored. 'I'm a magistrate. Stop!'

'It's Openshaw!' gasped Tankard, suddenly seeming to realise that he too had responsibilities as a magistrate.

He began to push his way past Dempsey when a gasp or a groan from the onlookers made it plain that something was amiss.

'He's lost his footing,' said Dempsey. 'He'll be trampled under the horses…'

But Tankard was already elbowing his way through the people.

'I'm a Justice of the Peace!' he bellowed in his tremendous voice. 'Halt! Stop!'

It was an urgent appeal, because the cavalry were moving forward on the crowd now, even though the rioters were already in flight. A close look at a cavalry charger and a mounted man with a heavy curved sabre in his hand was enough for them. Even the hardy ones were taking to their heels.

Tankard was badly buffeted as he tried to move against the tide of fugitives, but he succeeded in getting up to the first of the dragoons, who looked down at him stupidly from beneath their great helmets. None of them seemed to understand what was happening, but at any rate they had no orders to take offensive action. Not for the moment, apparently.

The vicar was still trying to find his footing amidst the confusing legs of a whole squadron of horses. Tankard seized him by the arm and pulled him up.

'Come on, Parson!'

Dempsey, Joe and Jeremy were close on his heels. Together they lifted the dazed man. There was a contusion on his temple where a hoof had caught it.

Tankard looked up at one of the dragoons.

'Where's your officer?' he demanded, but before the man could make any reply, there was another shout of alarm.

They looked down towards the Gable House, now almost hidden by smoke, and with only one or two figures at the entrance. Will was trying to shout something to them.

'What is it?' asked Dempsey.

'The old woman. She's gone back – into the blaze!'

'Fool!' raged Tankard. 'Couldn't you stop her?'

As he spoke, there came a high wailing scream.

'Oh, God!' gasped one of the burly dragoons, and his face showed the horror which gripped him.

The flames were tearing through the house unchecked. The heat drove everyone away. Robbie came up the road, shielding his face with his hands.

'She was mad,' he told them as he came up. 'Utterly mad!'

'She was calling for her mistress,' explained Will. 'Kept on calling for her. Then, as I let go of her arm, she dashed back – right into the fire. Had to save her mistress, she said.'

'Why!' said Robbie, shaking his head in sorrow. 'And her mistress has been dead all these long years!'

They stared stupidly into the inferno. The speed at which the fire had spread was incredible. The ancient dry timbers of the building had burned like tinder. The wind had fanned the flames, and now, as they looked, the whole roof came crashing down. It was a fearful sight. The horses shied and reared. Many of the men dismounted to try and pacify them. Sparks and hot fragments flew everywhere.

'It's over,' said Dempsey. 'Let us carry Mr Openshaw to safety.'

Sixteen: Moonshine and Lion are left

When the tumult had ceased, everybody in Penkley began to blame everybody else for what had happened. Reuben Tankard was one of the most vocal protestors of his own innocence.

He was quick to point out that of all the people in Penkley he had been the most ill-used and had suffered most. As a mill owner, his job was to spin cotton. This he had tried to do, and if he had been able to continue doing so, no one would have been out of work in the town, and no one would have been hungry – well, not unduly hungry. But it had become unprofitable to spin cotton. No one wanted it when spun. But it was not his fault that demand had collapsed after Bonaparte's defeat.

As for his having secretly employed Catchpole, this too was a perfectly justifiable action. Wasn't he a magistrate, entrusted with enforcing the laws of the land and preserving the King's Peace? Wasn't it his duty to be forewarned? Wouldn't he have been a fool to have neglected establishing some method of obtaining information?

Of course, it was unfortunate that Catchpole had turned out to be an unprincipled scoundrel. But was he – Tankard – to be held responsible for that? The blame lay on the spy's shoulders, and no one else's.

As for the uprising, what possible blame could attach to him? He had had no part in it. He was not privy to the plans of the conspirators. Dickinson and the embers of his Association must accept full blame for the rioting. Indeed, he was already considering whether to take action against them under the Combination Laws. Had they not contravened the statutes, three deaths would have been averted.

Tankard expounded his case with unaccustomed eloquence as he stood before the fire in the vicar's private room – for with the Gable House gutted, he and Jeremy had taken up temporary residence at the vicarage. Dempsey, whom he treated almost like an opposing counsel, sat in the vicar's chair and listened, fingering a flute as he did so. The two boys sat by the table, and every so often Caleb would slip quietly upstairs to see if his father needed anything.

Uncle Reuben had said much the same things ever since the disturbance had ended, but now, three days later, a new note was creeping in.

'I don't feel it's quite right,' he told Dempsey, 'and I'm saying this as a man, not as a magistrate – but bain't right for folks to suffer for what Woodrow might ha' done. Woodrow was a double-eyed villain, an' it's a pity his evil cannot die wi' him.'

Dempsey urged him to develop his argument.

'Maybe tha's guessed,' went on Uncle Reuben. 'I'm speakin' o' Joss Barker.'

'That's a matter for Quarter Sessions,' observed Dempsey.

'Aye, that it be. Yet Dickinson's made some arrangements wi' a lawyer, I believe.'

'I didn't know he'd made it so widely known,' returned the actor. 'He, too, is obsessed with the Combination Laws.'

Uncle Reuben nodded towards Caleb. 'I heard it from yon lad there.'

'In confidence,' Caleb reminded him.

'Aye, in confidence,' the mill owner assured him. 'But it seems as Barker'll need more than a lawyer, and it's really up to me and t' vicar. We it were as heard t' case, so happen we can scotch it. Perhaps a letter to t' chairman will explain it away.'

'Well,' said Dempsey. 'That would be very helpful, Mr Tankard, very helpful indeed. I share your feelings that Barker has been the victim of gross treachery—'

'He certainly was!' put in Caleb. 'Joss never meant any harm to anyone. He was the best of fellows. He—'

'Maybe,' growled the mill owner. 'I'm not sayin' he weren't. I'm not saying nowt, save that he'll have to learn to keep his mouth shut in future. It's one thing holding opinions. It's another to go shouting them about in taverns. If his spell in gaol's done nowt else, maybe it'll have taught him that.'

Dempsey played a few bars of an Irish jig on the flute.

'I would urge you, Mr Tankard,' he said, lowering the instrument for a moment, 'to do all you can in this matter, as nothing would more quickly restore a better feeling in the town. Bitterness is widespread, and folk are well aware that you were the one who hired the spy. They won't easily forgive.'

'Forgive?' asked Uncle Reuben. 'But it was they as started the whole thing. It was they who went plotting and scheming, breaking my windows—'

'There are two sides, however,' said Dempsey. 'Don't you think both sides have to do some forgiving?'

'I'll do all I can in the line o' duty,' snorted the mill owner. 'Look what I've done only today! Haven't I tried to put the parish administration on some sort of sound footing? Haven't I even given £100 of my own money to help people who were probably responsible for burning my house down and murdering my servant? Why! If that ain't turning the other cheek, what is?'

He looked round for some show of approval, expecting it evidently from Jeremy, if from no one else.

'Your servant wasn't murdered,' explained Dempsey. 'It's much better to get the facts right. She gave her life for a mistress she believed to be in danger.'

'Aye,' muttered Uncle Reuben, rather subdued by this statement of the case. 'But she was out of her mind.'

'Out of her mind or not,' Dempsey reminded him, softly, 'the sacrifice was exactly the same.'

No one spoke. Several moments passed.

'And in considering your £100,' went on Dempsey, 'let me tell you of a little incident which occurred last Saturday night. A man trudged up here through the snow – not a rich man – not by any means as rich as you are, Mr Tankard – and he brought his flute with him. And that bassoon over there. And some other objects which our worthy vicar had undertaken to pawn for a pound or two. This man, the pawnbroker, hadn't come for his money back. He wanted the vicar to retain the money, but he wanted to return the articles which had been pledged.'

Dempsey placed the flute to his lips and played another tune.

'There's a hard task here in Penkley,' he resumed, when the tune was concluded, 'a hard task in front of everyone. Many hard and heartbreaking decisions, maybe. I don't pretend to foretell how you'll overcome them. I don't even know whether – given the best will in the world – you ever will overcome them all. I'm an actor, not a mill owner, nor a millhand, so I can't advise. And I can well believe, Mr Tankard, that when it comes to running your business, you're the best man in Penkley to do it. I can well believe that Dickinson's ideas – on this subject – might be quite unrealistic. But that doesn't mean to say, Mr Tankard – with the greatest respect – that you shouldn't give his ideas a hearing.'

The mill owner grumbled something inaudible, something about engineers and men to their trade.

'Well,' cried Dempsey, springing out of his chair. 'It's getting late, and I'm on my way to Liverpool in the morning. I'd better go upstairs and see the vicar to bid him goodbye.'

The boys accompanied him. Mr Openshaw was propped up in bed, still looking pale and hollow cheeked. He brightened as his visitors entered.

'I've come to say goodbye, Vicar.'

The parson took the outstretched hand.

'I shall miss you. You've been a great help, Mr Bungeham – or whatever your name might be. I shall always think of you as Mr Bungeham, I can assure you.'

'And an excellent name it is,' declared Dempsey.

'So, Mr Bungeham, I mustn't let you go without thanking you a thousand times for all you have done here.'

'I've done very little,' smiled the actor. 'Just played a part as I normally do. It was you, sir, who, when everything seemed lost, gave hope to the townspeople.'

'Me? Hope to them?'

'The story has been told in Penkley – wherever two or three are gathered together – about what you did, sir. Of how you struggled from your sick-couch and threw yourself under the horses' hoofs in an attempt to avert bloodshed. It's made a great impression, Mr Openshaw.'

'Ah! But I didn't throw myself. I slipped in the snow.'

'What does it matter? You went out on their behalf. They realised you were prepared to put your preaching into practice.'

'But I am a very unworthy man, my friend. And not at all successful even in the pitiful things I attempt.'

'But let me tell you, Vicar, how profoundly you have influenced a poor actor, a mere strolling player,' said Dempsey, 'And I know you will continue to influence all who make your acquaintance. You are triumphantly successful when events have finished running their course, whatever appearances of failure there may have been during the running. And we all need your help and guidance. Take Caleb here, who scorns actors, so I'm told—'

'Not any more,' Caleb cut in, grinning.

'And Jeremy, who possibly still cherishes hopes—'

'I'll have to wait and see,' confessed Jeremy. 'My uncle needs me for the present. But later on…'

'So you see,' continued Dempsey, taking the vicar's hand again. 'There are hundreds of problems to be solved. But while you are struggling with them, I am afraid I shall be in fresh fields—'

'No, no!' The vicar corrected him with a smile. 'Fresh *woods* and pastures new.'

The End

Lightning Source UK Ltd.
Milton Keynes UK
UKOW042236210613

212661UK00001B/4/P